A MAJOR MIRACLE

Edward Donohue

Pen Press Publishers Ltd

© Edward Donohue 2007

All rights reserved

No part of this publication may be reproduced,
stored in a retrieval system, or transmitted
in any form or by any means, without
the prior permission in writing of the publisher,
nor be otherwise circulated in any form of binding or cover
other than that in which it is published and without a similar
condition including this condition being imposed on the
subsequent purchaser.

First published in Great Britain by
Pen Press Publishers Ltd
25 Eastern PLace
Brighton
BN2 1GJ

ISBN13: 978-1-905621-95-8

Printed and bound in the UK

A catalogue record of this book is available from
the British Library

Cover design by Jacqueline Abromeit

DEDICATION

This book is dedicated to the memory of Violet, Ian and Ben.
Whose lives were cut cruelly short.

ACKNOWLEDGEMENTS

I would like to thank my wife, Janet, for her advice and support, Maureen Brodie for her patient hard work and my son Guy for his technical assistance. Finally I would like to thank the staff of Pen Press for their advice and encouragement.

PREVIOUS TITLES

Edward Donohue is also the author of *Echoes in the Hills*, *Neither Pity Nor Patronise* and the children's title *Bravo Bunny to the Rescue*. His most recent publication is *Billy's Crowded Hour* which is set in the First World War.

CONTENTS

PREFACE	ix
CHAPTER ONE	1
CHAPTER TWO	4
CHAPTER THREE	9
CHAPTER FOUR	13
CHAPTER FIVE	17
CHAPTER SIX	20
CHAPTER SEVEN	24
CHAPTER EIGHT	28
CHAPTER NINE	31
CHAPTER TEN	34
CHAPTER ELEVEN	37
CHAPTER TWELVE	40
CHAPTER THIRTEEN	43
CHAPTER FOURTEEN	45
CHAPTER FIFTEEN	49
CHAPTER SIXTEEN	51
CHAPTER SEVENTEEN	54
CHAPTER EIGHTEEN	57
CHAPTER NINETEEN	60
CHAPTER TWENTY	62
CHAPTER TWENTY-ONE	64
CHAPTER TWENTY-TWO	67
CHAPTER TWENTY-THREE	69
CHAPTER TWENTY-FOUR	72
CHAPTER TWENTY-FIVE	75
CHAPTER TWENTY-SIX	77
CHAPTER TWENTY-SEVEN	79
CHAPTER TWENTY-EIGHT	81
CHAPTER TWENTY-NINE	85
CHAPTER THIRTY	88
CHAPTER THIRTY-ONE	90

CHAPTER THIRTY-TWO	92
CHAPTER THIRTY-THREE	94
CHAPTER THIRTY-FOUR	96
CHAPTER THIRTY-FIVE	98
CHAPTER THIRTY-SIX	101
CHAPTER THIRTY-SEVEN	104
CHAPTER THIRTY-EIGHT	107
CHAPTER THIRTY-NINE	109
CHAPTER FORTY	111
CHAPTER FORTY-ONE	113
CHAPTER FORTY-TWO	115
CHAPTER FORTY-THREE	119
CHAPTER FORTY-FOUR	122
CHAPTER FORTY-FIVE	124
CHAPTER FORTY-SIX	126
CHAPTER FORTY-SEVEN	128
CHAPTER FORTY-EIGHT	130
CHAPTER FORTY-NINE	133
CHAPTER FIFTY	135
CHAPTER FIFTY-ONE	137
CHAPTER FIFTY-TWO	139
CHAPTER FIFTY-THREE	141
CHAPTER FIFTY-FOUR	143
CHAPTER FIFTY-FIVE	145
CHAPTER FIFTY-SIX	148
CHAPTER FIFTY-SEVEN	151
CHAPTER FIFTY-EIGHT	154
CHAPTER FIFTY-NINE	157
CHAPTER SIXTY	160
CHAPTER SIXTY-ONE	162
CHAPTER SIXTY-TWO	165
CHAPTER SIXTY-THREE	168
CHAPTER SIXTY-FOUR	170
CHAPTER SIXTY-FIVE	172
AUTHOR'S NOTES	175

PREFACE

Many years ago there was a saying which went 'Don't put your daughter on the stage Mrs. Worthington.' Perhaps we could adapt that saying to 'Don't put your parent in a home Mrs. Worthington.' At least not until you have fully acquainted yourself with it. Too many parents who have loved and cherished their children all their lives suddenly find themselves abandoned in residential care. Obviously there are often explicable reasons for this, physical infirmity, mental confusion or simply the inability of the family to offer a viable alternative.

Nevertheless, when people who have been valued members of society suddenly find themselves vulnerable and unwanted it may seem to them that the whole of their life has been wasted. On the other hand it may well be that the quality of life offered in a good residential home can prove beneficial. Because one enters the final years of ones life it does not have to mean simply waiting to die. It may and should mean beginning another phase of life which can be exciting and stimulating.

There are homes like Hollytree House and the Haven and many others shades of home between these two. Anybody who is contemplating moving a loved one into a residential setting should inspect the premises very carefully, see the menu book, the activities diary and even more importantly, meet the staff. Any home which will not divulge this information may well be not suitable. Some people will argue that local authority homes are better than private homes while other people will firmly assert the opposite. It is clearly in the interest of the potential resident to look at both alternatives in their particular area. Obviously the manager or proprietor is a key person and their attitude and ideas will influence the kind of life offered to the residents.

The author has encountered several hundred residential care workers during his time as a lecturer and social work advisor. He has no hesitation in asserting that the vast majority are caring and dedicated people but there is always a small minority who don't particularly care and who are capable of either verbal or physical abuse.

Similarly he has worked with many social workers who are also conscientious and committed to the care of their clients. Again however, there is a small minority who seem to abuse the power given to them by society.

It would be nice to think that the reader will enjoy the book which follows but accept the premise that there are always possible dangers and pitfalls lurking in a residential home. If you must put your parent in a home Mrs. Worthington please ensure that it is the right home for them.

CHAPTER ONE

As the Major walked with his son, George, through the front door of the residential home known as the Haven, his first impression was the smell, an unpleasant mixture of cooked vegetables, urine and misery. 'What the devil am I doing here,' he thought, but then immediately admitted to himself that he knew only too well. His wife of forty-seven years had died suddenly a few months ago and he had spent the intervening period living with his son and his daughter-in-law, not a happy experience.

His daughter-in-law was fiercely house-proud and for that reason, had never had any children of her own. The Major had endured months of having cushions straightened as soon as he stood up, books and newspapers put away before he had finished reading them and generally being made to feel unwelcome and unwanted. Eventually he and George had sat down and discussed the problem of his future. George had admitted that it was very unlikely that Isabel, his wife, would ever fully accept her father-in-law into her home. He could not afford to buy a place of his own because he had mortgaged his previous home to the hilt when he was trying to preserve his business. This ultimately failed anyway and he was left with very little in the way of capital.

George had explained that he had a friend, Jack Smith, who was in partnership with a Mr Khan and they owned two residential homes for the elderly. One of the homes, Hollytree

House, had no vacancies at the present time but there was a vacancy at the Haven. George was sure that his friendship with Jack Smith would enable them to negotiate a discounted fee. At the time the Major thought that anywhere would be preferable to living with Isabel but now he was not so sure.

At this point his thoughts were broken by the arrival of a large-bosomed imposing woman who introduced herself as Donna, the manager. She was accompanied by a small rather scrawny man whom she introduced as Denis, her deputy. The Major took an immediate and probably unreasonable dislike to Denis who was losing his hair at the front and compensated by having a bunch of hair tied with a bow at the back.

After the brief introduction Donna ignored the Major and spoke directly to his son. She asked whether he was fussy about his food and whether he slept through the night. She said this latter point was very important because the night care staff had more than enough problems at the moment. George answered without enthusiasm and said that he was sure his father was able to speak for himself. After a few more minutes of desultory conversation Donna said that Denis would show the Major to his room and that tea would be at five-thirty. George and his father made their farewells and it was obvious that George could not wait to take his leave.

The Major followed Denis up a wide staircase and then along a narrow and rather dimly lit corridor. Denis opened a door at the far end and said, 'OK old chap, this is where you'll sleep.' The room was quite pleasant with two windows and a three-quarter-size bed. 'I'm sure you will like it here,' said Denis, in a tone that suggested complete indifference, and he went out shutting the door.

The Major sat on the only chair in the room and thought, 'So this is what it has been all about. Twenty-seven years in the army and thirty years running my own small printing firm and now I finish up in, of all places, a dreary home called the Haven.'

He had been a good but not particularly distinguished soldier. He never rose beyond the rank of Major, however he had been in the Normandy invasion and later saw service in Korea and the Middle East. He and Angela got married while he was a young soldier. They only had the one child, George, but he would certainly have described their marriage as a happy one. He sat there for a long time thinking about his wife, Angela, whom he had loved very much. It was doubly unfortunate that after struggling for some time with his printing business he had had to admit defeat; there was no way he could compete with the bigger firms and modern technology, so he was forced to close down.

He and Angela then started to plan a cruise for a holiday and both of them were looking forward to this. One lunch time, and completely without warning, she had a heart attack and collapsed while taking a rice pudding out of the oven. The Major had called for an ambulance but she was already dead when it arrived. Somehow she had managed to place the pudding bowl unbroken on the floor and he picked up the pudding and kept it on the kitchen table for several weeks before eventually, and reluctantly, throwing it away.

Just before five-thirty he shook himself out of his reverie and went downstairs to find the dining room. In it there were two long tables with twelve places on each, most of the occupants were already seated and when the Major said good evening he got one or two mumbled responses. He sat in one of the three empty spaces and waited for his first meal in the Haven.

CHAPTER TWO

After dinner he felt that he was not ready to face the lounge and the inevitable television and so he returned to his own room. Dinner, or tea as the care staff called it, had done nothing to raise his spirits. It had been rather coagulated beans on toast followed by jelly and custard, which compared very unfavourably with his wife, Angela's, cooking. He had sat opposite a woman who managed to get most of her food into her mouth but a fair proportion of it on her face and clothes. One of the two care staff on duty had addressed her as Elsie and tried to help her but Elsie kept pushing her away whilst grinning somewhat vacantly at the Major.

Most of the other residents just got on with their food and there was very little conversation. The exception was between the two care staff on duty, who referred to each other as Mary and Rose, and talked as if the residents were either deaf or not present. Mary said, 'I will be glad when it's nine o'clock, I've had just about enough of this lot today.'

Rose nodded in agreement then said, 'If I didn't need the money I would tell them where to stick their job, I hate working in this dump.' After the meal Rose told him that there would be a supper drink at nine o'clock in the lounge.

He went down just before nine deluding himself that perhaps a supper drink could mean a whisky and soda; however he found that the alternatives were tea or cocoa and he sipped a cup of the latter without enthusiasm. About half past nine

Denis came into the lounge and announced that it was time for the residents to go to their rooms. The Major went upstairs and started to get ready for bed. 'It's just like school,' he mused, because he had boarded at a very minor public school and he couldn't help thinking how the clock had turned full circle and he was back to childhood. He slept very fitfully that night and was disturbed by a lot of strange noises and some shouting.

*

The following morning, breakfast was even more subdued than dinner had been the night before. The Major noticed that there were two empty places and overheard Rose telling another care worker that the two missing residents 'weren't in for breakfast because they had messed their beds'.

After breakfast the Major decided that he would go for a walk. As he was going out of the front door Denis stopped him and asked him where he was going. He said that as it was such a nice morning he thought he would go and find a newspaper shop and buy himself a paper. Denis said, 'That's a good idea, perhaps you will be kind enough to get me a copy of the Daily Mirror and bring it back for me.' The Major agreed and set off to find the shops.

When he returned he looked for Denis and one of the care staff told him that he lived in a caravan at the bottom of the garden and would probably be down there. The Major strolled down the garden, which was rather neglected and overgrown, and knocked on the caravan door. When Denis opened the door there was a waft of rather sweet and sickly cigarette smoke, which made the Major immediately think of hippies and pot. 'Thank you old chap,' said Denis, taking the paper but not offering to pay for it.

The Major returned to the house and spent the morning studying the horse racing, something which had been one of his favourite hobbies in recent years. He was not an avid gambler and never lost more than a few pounds, but he did enjoy watching racing on the television and in the past had attended quite a few race meetings. There was coffee at eleven o'clock and lunch followed promptly at one. Unfortunately it was no more inspiring than dinner had been, cottage pie followed by some kind of watery milk pudding.

After lunch the Major walked down to a betting office, which he had noticed that morning, and proceeded to back three of his selections. Unfortunately his selection had obviously been influenced by his mood and all of them were un-placed.

The evening meal was depressing; there was a slight variation as this time it was sardines on toast. He heard the care staff grumbling; it was the same pair as yesterday, Rose and Mary. They were complaining that they had to do the teas because there was now only one cook who came in the mornings. Rose said, 'We're short of staff because they want to save money.'

'Perhaps they're saving up to get married,' Mary replied. This apparently had something to do with Donna and Denis saving money. 'She's down at his caravan now, counselling him,' one said, and they both sniggered.

Rose continued, 'We're also supposed to do the cleaning at the moment. She sacked Marjorie because she said that she used to answer back and was a malicious gossip but really it was probably a question of saving more money.' This possibly accounted for the rather neglected appearance of the rooms and the unpleasant odours which permeated the house.

The evening dragged slowly by. The Major watched *The Bill* with one eye whilst reading his paper and then it was nine o'clock and drinks time.

The evening before he had noticed two members of the

care staff dispensing pills and small quantities of liquid. This evening one of the staff, Mary, approached him and asked what medication he was on. He was surprised but he replied, 'None, apart from the occasional painkiller when I have a headache or pains in my back.'

'All the residents take medication,' she said, 'it helps them to sleep, are you sure you wouldn't like something?'

'No thank you,' replied the Major. 'In any case shouldn't the doctor prescribe medication?' She said that there was always plenty in stock because when people died or moved the medication wasn't thrown away.

'Usually the manager or Denis decides on what medication we should give out.'

The Major was puzzled and he asked whether there should be records about this.

'Oh there are,' was the reply, 'but what we do and what we write down might be quite different.'

Just then the manager appeared and asked the Major if he was settling in. 'You will soon get used to our routine,' she said, 'and I'm sure you will be happy here.' The Major was not so sure.

That night he got up to go to the lavatory some time just after midnight. As he was passing one of the bedroom doors he heard what sounded like two slaps followed by sobbing. Then somebody said, 'the dirty cow has shit herself again, we will have to stick her in the bath.'

A second voice said, 'The water is not very warm.'

'Serves her right,' said the first voice, 'perhaps it will teach her not to be so disgusting.'

The Major went to the lavatory and as he was returning one of the night care staff was coming out of the bedroom door from which he had heard the noises.

'What the hell are you doing wandering about,' she said, 'you should be in your room.'

'I presume that I am allowed to go the lavatory,' the Major replied.

'Oh go and get into your bed, you silly old fool,' she retorted.

The Major lay in bed thinking that it would be impossible for him to cope with the sort of things which went on in the home. He decided that the following morning he would speak to the manager, although he felt little optimism about the outcome. Lying in the inhospitable home made him think again of Angela and the happy times they had enjoyed together. With his military training he prided himself as a man who had complete control over his emotions, nevertheless as he lay there he felt a prickling at the back of his eyes and an unwelcome tear trickling down his cheek. He wondered again why his beloved wife had been taken from him so suddenly and without warning. 'Why did you leave me Angela?' he cried aloud. 'Will I ever know happiness again,' he wondered, before dropping off into an uneasy sleep.

CHAPTER THREE

The following morning it was raining heavily and after a breakfast consisting of porridge, followed by sausage and beans, the Major went and knocked on the manager's door. When she opened the door he said that he would like to speak to her about some matters which concerned him. 'Yes,' she said, 'I've read the night care staff report. Perhaps you will be good enough to come back at eleven o'clock when Denis is on duty and we can see you together.'

The Major went back to his room and started to read one of the books that he had brought with him. He couldn't settle and spent most of the time looking at the rain beating against the windows. At eleven o'clock he went downstairs and presented himself at the manager's door. After he knocked Denis opened the door and asked him to come in and sit down. Denis and Donna were sitting on the other side of the desk drinking coffee but did not offer to give him any.

'Right,' said Donna, 'let us hear what you have to say.'

The Major recounted the events of the night before, saying that he was very disturbed by what he had heard coming from the room and not at all happy about the way in which he had been spoken to.

'Well,' replied Donna, 'I have read the report written by the night staff and their version is somewhat different. It is true that Mrs Higgins had got herself into a bit of a mess but the staff got her up, gave her a bath and changed her bed; there was certainly no question of slapping or crying or tepid bath water, you must have completely misheard this.'

'My hearing is perfectly good,' replied the Major, 'and in any case, what about the way the care staff spoke to me?'

'I accept that they were probably a bit harassed and they were also rather disturbed by the fact that you were hanging around the women's rooms in the middle of the night. They don't know you and obviously they had no idea about what you were doing.'

'So it's just a question of my word against theirs?' said the Major.

'Well you could say that,' said Donna, 'but these girls have worked with me for some time and obviously I have to believe them. Perhaps you were tired and not properly awake and therefore misunderstood everything.'

At that point, Denis, who had been completely silent, said, 'You had better hurry along to the lounge, Major, or you will miss your morning coffee.'

The Major stood up, feeling far from happy, and left the office.

He thought, 'To hell with the morning coffee, I'll get my coat and umbrella and go into town.' He pottered around town for the rest of the morning and then decided to treat himself to a sandwich and a whisky and soda in one of the several pubs. The pub was quite busy and the Major felt it was a relief to sit among normal people and hear ordinary, everyday conversation. Eventually he finished his simple lunch and walked back to the Haven.

When he got there he was greeted by Denis, who said, 'Where on earth have you been? If you are going to miss a meal we need to know in advance.'

'I am sure that the chef was highly disappointed that one of her gourmet meals was wasted,' replied the Major, and he walked upstairs.

'There's no need for sarcasm,' shouted Denis, and he went off to the office.

Later that afternoon, Jack Smith, one of the owners, came to the Haven in response to a telephone call from Donna. She and Denis met with him in the office and announced that they felt the Major had been wrongly placed with them.

'You know how it is, Jack; we prefer to have the simple ones here. Why wasn't Major Webb placed at Hollytree House?'

'The quick answer to that,' replied Jack Smith, 'is that there wasn't a vacancy and it doesn't look as if there will be one for some time, as all the residents appear healthy.'

Denis suggested that perhaps there could be an exchange; maybe there was somebody at Hollytree House who wasn't too much trouble and could be transferred to the Haven.

'I don't know about that,' said Jack Smith, 'you know how Tricia, the manager, is very protective of her residents and wouldn't want one of them moved for the wrong reason.'

Donna then said, 'Yes, but you're the boss and if you tell her that an exchange has to take place then I don't see how she can refuse.'

Jack Smith said that they should leave the matter with him and he would see what he could do.

'As soon as possible then,' said Donna, 'otherwise that man is going to cause an awful lot of trouble.'

That night the Major was preparing for bed and he made his way to where the two bathrooms used for the men were, opposite to each other. As he drew near he heard loud voices and laughter. Standing in the corridor outside the bathrooms were Denis and Arnold, one of the night staff. They were both clutching the arms of two elderly residents who were completely naked.

'Just look at the todger on this one,' said Arnold.

'Very impressive,' said Denis, 'but look at the balls on Percy, he must have been a real stallion in his youth.'

Both the old men looked confused and bewildered and one looked very close to tears. The Major could not prevent himself from saying, 'What the devil is going on?'

'More to the point,' said Denis angrily, 'what the hell has it got to do with you?'

'You're making fun of two helpless old men and I think that is both despicable and indecent,' replied the Major.

Denis's response was to say, 'Come on, Arnold' let's put these two to bed and ignore the galloping Major.'

*

The following morning the Major again asked to see the manager. Once again she told him that he had clearly misunderstood, and in any case he seemed determined to cause trouble. 'You are obviously not happy here,' she said, 'and I am trying to arrange a transfer for you.'

Two days later Jack Smith returned to the Haven and told them that he had persuaded Tricia to move a resident called Horace Slocombe from Hollytree House to the Haven. 'The poor old chap can only move around with a walking frame and so he will obviously mean more physical work for your staff,' he said. Both Donna and Denis assured Jack Smith that they would rather have work than troublemakers.

'After all,' said Denis, 'one wrinkly is much the same as another and the quiet ones are the easiest.'

Thus the transfer was arranged.

CHAPTER FOUR

The following day the Major was told that he was moving to Hollytree House. 'I'll take you up this afternoon,' said Denis.

'No thanks,' said the Major. 'I'm going into town this morning and I'll have a spot of lunch there. After lunch I will take myself to Hollytree House and you can arrange to move my luggage.'

'Suits me,' said Denis. 'I'll be glad to see the back of you.'

The Major pottered around town and had his usual lunch of a sandwich and a whisky and soda. He then made his way slowly and very reluctantly to Hollytree House.

He was pleasantly surprised by the garden, which even in October was still very colourful. He arrived at the front door, which was slightly ajar, and ringing the bell, he went in. He suddenly had a sense of déjà vu because there was a smell. However, his brain quickly registered the fact that this was a smell of furniture polish, flowers and warmth because on a table in the hall was a vase containing roses. At the sound of the bell, a smiling, blonde, young woman appeared who introduced herself as Tricia Beasley, the manager. 'You must be Major Webb,' she said. 'We've been looking forward to your arrival.'

He followed her into her office, which was bright and very tidy and she asked him to sit down. 'Tell me something about yourself,' she said, 'the kind of things you like doing for example.' They chatted for a while and then she said, 'Do you have a favourite meal?' The Major replied that his tastes were relatively simple and would she believe that his favourite meal was egg and chips. 'Oh,' replied Tricia, 'that is very popular here.' Just then a small, dark haired young woman came into the room and Tricia introduced her as her deputy, Paula. 'Paula will show you to your room and I'll look forward to seeing you later,' said Tricia.

The Major followed Paula up the stairs and onto a nicely decorated landing where there were several doors. She took him into a light, airy room, which was at the back of the house and looked out onto an immaculate garden. 'What a lovely garden,' he said.

'Yes,' replied Paula, 'Tricia is very keen on the garden and we all help.' She then said that there would be a cup of tea in the lounge at about four o'clock and she hoped that he would come down for that. The Major unpacked, because his luggage had obviously been delivered earlier by Denis, and stood in the middle of the room. He was impressed that the room seemed as clean and polished as the rest of the house and he found himself thinking, 'I may well like it here.'

When he'd finished unpacking he went down to the lounge, where to his surprise, the television was not on. There were a group of ladies sitting round a table at the window who appeared to be playing bridge, two or three other people scattered around reading and two men playing chess. Several of them looked up and smiled when he went in, but he heard music coming from an adjoining room so he went over and looked through into what obviously was a music room. There was a man with long silver hair playing the piano and the Major stood and listened to a medley of tunes dating back to the 1930's and 40's.

The man suddenly realised the Major was standing by the

door and he stood up and said, 'Hello, old boy, I'm just tickling the ivories, my name's Jerry.'

'How do you do,' said the Major, 'I'm Major Webb, but my friends call me Harry.'

'Well,' said Jerry, 'let's go and have a cup of tea and I'll introduce you to some of the others.' He led the Major first towards the chess players and said, 'These are my mates, Vic and Glyn; we have a small liar dice club which you may care to join once you've settled in. Horace, the chap who moved, used to play, but I'm afraid that in the last few weeks he got very forgetful.' 'Mind you,' he went on, 'he was an ex teacher and never one of the sharpest knives in the box.'

He then took the Major over to the ladies sitting around the bridge table and introduced them as Harriet, Joyce, Willy and Poppy. The lady he called Willy said, 'Actually, my name is Wilhelmina, but I've always been called Willy.' Jerry introduced the Major to several more people but he couldn't remember all their names, and then one of the staff came in pushing the tea trolley, which not only contained tea, but also several plates with scones and cakes. The next two hours passed very quickly, the Major chatted to most of the other residents. He learned that there were twenty residents in all: eight men and twelve ladies. Most of them seemed very lively and outgoing in direct contrast to the residents of the Haven.

Suddenly there was a loud booming sound from the hall, which indicated that somebody was beating the dinner gong with some enthusiasm. He went into the dining room with Jerry and instead of two long tables saw that there were six tables, each containing four places. 'You had better come and sit with us,' said Jerry. 'We have a space now that Horace has gone.'

The Major realised that in addition to the residents the sixth table was intended for members of staff who actually ate with the residents, as opposed to in the Haven, where the staff had a separate dining room. Tricia, the manager, introduced the Major to everybody, making a small speech of welcome and she said with a smile, 'We're having egg and chips in his honour.' For a moment the Major was almost overwhelmed by this small but significant gesture, he felt so welcome that he didn't know quite what to say so he contented himself by standing up smiling and saying, 'Thank you, Tricia, I'm very glad to be here.' The chips were lightly browned and crisp, the eggs were slightly crisp on the outside and the yolks were soft and runny just like Angela used to cook them. As he started to eat his first meal at Hollytree House he could have sworn he heard Angela say, 'Enjoy your meal, darling,' just as she had so many times before.

CHAPTER FIVE

After dinner the Major asked Tricia if they could have another brief chat. He explained that he was worried about having taken somebody's place in order to be in Hollytree House. Tricia assured him that he really did not need to worry as Horace Slocombe, his predecessor, not only needed a Zimmer frame but he had been steadily losing his memory and would be almost oblivious to his surroundings. 'That's all very well,' said the Major, 'but will he be looked after properly in the Haven?' Tricia replied that it was not for her to criticise her colleagues in the other home but she knew that they were probably better at looking after the less able than catering for the needs of somebody like the Major.

She then said, 'If I may speak to you confidentially…'

'Of course,' replied the Major.

Tricia continued '…poor Horace had become very confused and started to wander into the ladies' bathrooms even when they were in use, he had become something of an embarrassment.' She went on to say that she had received a report from the Haven and knew that the Major had not settled in there. 'However,' she assured him, 'the report has no relevance to us and we will judge you entirely on the way you respond here.' The Major felt reassured by this and went back to the lounge in a much happier frame of mind.

There he was introduced to the liar dice club; it was a game which was vaguely familiar to him as it used to be played in the officers' mess when he was in the army. It was played with five poker dice and was based on the concept of bluff and counter bluff. It did not take the Major long to realise that he was up against real experts and was the first player to be eliminated in every game. He learned a little more about his companions. Vic was sometimes referred to as the Professor because he had been a university lecturer; he was still a handsome man despite being in his mid seventies. Glyn was known as the Commodore because he had once been in the Navy; he was a large man with a red face and a sparse covering of white hair. Jerry had spent most of his life in advertising but he didn't have a nickname and was generally regarded as the self-appointed leader of the group. He was a dapper man who was never seen without a collar and tie or a cravat.

The Major learned that Glyn had never been married and that Vic and Jerry had lost their wives some years earlier. His new companions also gave him some more information about the staff. They all thought that Tricia was a great manager. 'A bit keen on the spit and polish,' Jerry said, 'but she doesn't ask anybody to do anything she isn't prepared to do herself.' Paula, the little sparrow-like lady, was always good-natured and arranged quite a lot of interesting outings. 'Then, of course,' they said, 'there's Bridie,' and they all smiled and said, 'we'll tell you about her when you've been here a little longer.'

They said that most of the other residents were easy to get on with and there was a good spirit of camaraderie. 'A couple of the ladies can be a bit touchy. Mrs Harrington-Ford, for example, always has to be referred to formally by her surname and her friend Millicent is inclined to be a bit of a busybody, but they're fairly harmless really.'

Again the evening seemed to pass very quickly and at about nine-thirty the trolley came in for supper drinks.

He was interested to observe that there was no medication trolley. He asked Jerry about this and Jerry replied that as far as he knew there were very few residents on regular medication. 'Mind you,' he said, 'I've heard of a number of homes where they use what they laughingly call the "medical cosh".' When the Major raised his eyebrows Jerry went on to explain that in order to keep residents quiet and subdued they were given drugs which had been designed for much more disturbed people. He went on to say that in Hollytree House Paula or Tricia always saw the residents individually if they need any medicine. 'What time's curfew then?' asked the Major, only too aware of the rules at the Haven.

'Oh there's no particular time for going up,' he was told, 'but we have an understanding that we are usually all in our rooms by eleven unless we've got some sort of activity on or some of us are watching something very late on the television.' The Major went up to his room at about ten-thirty, bidding the others goodnight and that night, for the first time in a long time, he slept soundly all through the night.

CHAPTER SIX

The first week at Hollytree House was so different from his stay at the Haven that the Major could not believe they were both under the same ownership. As he settled in he got to know the staff quite quickly. Mrs Burton was the cook responsible for breakfasts and lunches, and Mrs Halliday, who said 'please call me Amy', was responsible for teas and dinners. Lucy was a bright, chatty young woman who was responsible for most of the cleaning. However, most of the residents seemed to keep their own rooms clean and tidy. The one exception to this was Jerry, who said that he was far too old to start doing women's work.

The gardens were kept in order by a part time gardener called Andy; he was a pleasant young man who was always happy to talk to the residents and accept any help that they offered. The Major noticed that Andy was very adept at keeping a straight face when some of the advice proffered to him was a little bizarre. Apart from Tricia and Paula there were five other care staff. Jean was an older lady with a very kind manner who addressed everyone as m'dear. Bridie was a dark-haired, pretty young woman who spoke with an Irish accent and always had a smile for the residents, although the Major later learned that her home life was far from happy.

June and Edna were two women in their forties who were quiet and efficient. Finally, there was Tim who was designated the third in charge and whose main responsibility was to look after the maintenance of the building. Tim had shoulder-length hair and he had apparently told Jerry that he once had to do three months in prison for possessing cannabis. In prison they had cut off all his hair and when he came out he vowed that he would never have his hair cut again. They seemed to be a happy staff group and gave the impression that they were genuinely concerned for the welfare of the residents.

There were also three night staff who worked on a rota basis and in addition each night there would be one of the day staff sleeping in. Their caring attitudes seemed to be in direct contrast to the behaviour of the staff in the Haven. The Major learned that Paula, the deputy manager, arranged an outing for the residents once a fortnight. Those residents who wanted to go usually travelled in the sixteen-seater minibus, but if there were more than fourteen residents and two staff then Tricia's car carried the extra people.

Every Thursday evening the liar dice team, as the Major thought of them, had an evening out at the local pub called the Black Swan. The publican was a large, cheerful man called Les and he always saved a corner table for them and was perhaps a little more than generous with the size of their drinks. The first Thursday they invited the Major to join them and they introduced him to Les. 'Pleased to meet you,' said Les, 'I always think of these lads as grumpy old men putting the world to rights.'

'Well,' said Vic, 'I think that by the time we have reached our age we have a right to express our own views and opinions.'

Les said that he couldn't agree more. 'You do have every right.'

They got their drinks and after a few games of the inevitable liar dice the talk turned to gambling in general. Glyn and Jerry had once been to Las Vegas and thought rather wistfully that it would be nice to go again. Jerry said that at their age the problem was not the destination but the trials and tribulations of getting there. He went on to say he once loved travelling but now it all seemed too much effort.

The Major talked about his interest in horse racing. He explained that each year he had four ambitions. He wanted to win the autumn double, which were two races called the Cambridgeshire and the Cesarewitch; the spring double, which was the Lincoln Handicap and the Grand National; the Derby/Oaks double and perhaps most of all, the bet he referred to as the Cheltenham four.

'What is the Cheltenham four?' asked Vic.

The Major explained that it was an accumulator bet on the Champion Hurdle, the Champion Chase, the Triumph Hurdle and the Gold Cup. He told them that he had all the three doubles up in the past but he'd never managed to complete the four timer.

He went on to say that the autumn double was due in the next two weeks. The Cambridgeshire would be run on the coming Saturday and the Cesarewitch was two weeks later. He said that if they each put in ten pounds he could place a twenty-pound each way double and they could share the proceeds. Glyn was rather sceptical and Vic said he had always thought that backing horses was a bit of a mugs game. Jerry interceded and said, 'Come on, chaps, ten pounds is hardly a fortune and it would be a bit of interest.'

Eventually they agreed and asked Harry, as they were now all calling him, what his selections were. He said that he wanted to back a horse called She's Our Mare in the Cambridgeshire and a horse called Top Cees in the Cesarewitch. 'It's a bit long in the tooth for a flat horse,' he said, 'as it's nine years old but the Cesarewitch is a stayer's race and I think it's got a good chance.'

Vic said, 'If you find these winners for us perhaps we'll join you in an attempt at the Cheltenham four.' Little did they realise just how significant that remark would become in a few months time and how much they would depend on Harry's skill and Lady Luck. They decided it was time to return to Hollytree House and they said their goodbyes to Les. 'Goodnight lads,' he replied, 'take care and don't do anything I wouldn't do.'

CHAPTER SEVEN

In one of those strange coincidences of fate there was a meeting taking place in a public house on the other side of the city which was, to say the least, relevant to the future of Hollytree House. Three men were huddled round a small table and a casual observer may well have been reminded of the three witches in the opening scene of *Macbeth*. Certainly the way they huddled together looked distinctly conspiratorial. One was Jack Smith, the co-owner of the Haven and Hollytree House. He was a bald ruddy-faced man with a bushy, grey moustache. He was wearing a rather battered sports coat and an open necked shirt. He was probably about three stone heavier than he ought to have been. The second man was a solicitor, Reuben Jones, and he too was almost bald but had a few strands of hair carefully arranged across his head. He was wearing a smart pin striped suit and a tie which obviously represented some minor public school. The third man was tall and thin and he sported a narrow, black moustache over a mouth which seemed to be set in a permanent sneer. He was wearing a nondescript grey suit and a bright red polka dotted tie. His name was James Slighe and he had a job working for the local Social Services Department.

These three gentlemen had spent the earlier part of the evening at one of their society's meetings and had gathered afterwards in the public house at the request of Reuben Jones.

'What's all this about then, Reuben?' asked Jack Smith.

Reuben Jones said, 'Before I start I want to be assured that this conversation is completely confidential.'

Smith replied, 'No problem with me, I always know when to keep my mouth shut.'

James Slighe also indicated that as far as he too was concerned the meeting would remain completely confidential.

Reuben Jones then went on to tell them that he had a very wealthy client who was a property developer and builder, he had just received planning permission to build twenty houses along Portland Road.

'But that's where my place, Hollytree House, is.' said Jack Smith.

'Exactly,' replied Reuben, 'the land in question is actually adjacent to your property, which I believe is about four acres in total.'

'Nearer five,' said Jack Smith, 'but of course we have got the old people's home right in the middle.'

'Quite,' replied Jones, 'but if we had another five acres to offer to my property developer friend it would probably be worth as much as three million pounds.'

The three men sat sipping their drinks and thinking about this relatively large sum of money. James Slighe spoke for the first time and said, 'This is all very interesting but I don't see how I come into the equation.'

'Ah,' said Reuben, 'if Jack just closed his old peoples' home to sell the land, then there would be a public outcry and possibly planning permission would be refused. But if the Social Services Department closed the home down then the land could be sold legitimately.'

'There's one major snag,' said Jack Smith. 'My fellow owner, Mr Khan, would never agree to closing the home because his mother started it and she made him promise that he would always keep it open. I know for a fact that he wants to retire and go back to Pakistan in the future but I am certain that he wouldn't sell the home unless there were legal safeguards for keeping it open.'

'Right again,' said Reuben, 'which is another reason for getting the home closed down by the authorities.'

'Could you do it, James?' he said, turning to Slighe, who thought for a while and then replied that he was sure it could be arranged without too much difficulty.

'It wouldn't be the first time we have closed a home, although never for three million pounds,' he said, with an unpleasant smirk.

Reuben Jones then said, 'Well there is no need for us to make a decision right at this moment, but time is of the essence because my developer friend would need to know that he had acquired the land before he starts building on the other section.'

The three conspirators agreed to mull it over and meet in a week's time. After making their farewells each went in their respective directions home.

*

Meanwhile, the Major was still worrying about the residents he had left behind at the Haven. He felt he should do something, so decided to write to the Director of Social Services and the local Member of Parliament. He wasn't optimistic; he had been involved with at least three sections of the local authority over the years and had a very poor opinion of them.

The Education Department was staffed by failed teachers looking for an easy alternative, the Highways Department was incompetent and wasted huge amounts of money, and the Social Services Department was full of people with more problems than their clients. The one thing they all had in common was the desire to work from nine to five for five days a week with substantial holidays and an openly abused sick leave system. The Major doubted whether many people employed in his local authority had any concern for the people they were supposed to serve, their chief ambition being a comfortable pension at the end of a fairly easy working life. 'Still,' he mused, 'perhaps I have just been unfortunate with this particular local authority; it may be much better in other parts of the country.' But he wasn't convinced.

The local MP who had been sitting for many years was one Alistair Dunne, known to his friends and constituents as 'Fat Al', which neatly summed up how people regarded him. The Major's lack of expectation was confirmed. The MP wrote a bland letter saying he would pass the Major's concerns onto the appropriate authorities. The Director of Social Services did not even acknowledge the letter.

CHAPTER EIGHT

On Saturday morning breakfast was a lively affair at Hollytree House. There was much animated discussion about the first leg of the autumn double, which was due to take place that afternoon. Jerry asked the Major how he was going to go about placing the bet and the Major replied, 'If you all give me your ten pounds I will go down to the bookmakers after breakfast and place the bet.' Glyn, Jerry and Vic all produced a ten-pound note and the Major tucked them away in his wallet. The ladies at the next table overheard the conversation and were very curious so Jerry walked over and explained exactly what was going on.

Harriet said that she was partial to a bit of a flutter herself and could she join in the bet. Jerry explained that this was just a first time experiment and perhaps in future she could join in. 'Bear in mind,' he said, 'if we win then we'll all have a jolly good party and you will benefit that way.'

After breakfast the Major walked purposefully down into town and decided that he would place a ten pound each way double in the two different bookmakers that he frequented, thus, he hoped, taking money from both. Afterwards, on the way back, he went and had his usual whisky and soda. On his return he assured his fellow residents that the bet had been placed.

After lunch they all assembled in the lounge and Tricia, sensing the air of excitement, asked what was going on. Jerry explained to Tricia that he and the other men were just having a small bet on a race at Newmarket that afternoon. Just before three o'clock most of the residents assembled in the lounge and waited eagerly for the race to begin.

Vic said, 'Which one is the horse we're on?' And the Major pointed out the horse called She's Our Mare.

'Looks a bit small to me,' said Glyn, 'some of the other horses are a lot bigger.' The Major assured him that size wasn't everything and he had studied the form carefully. He was reasonably confident that they were on the right horse.

All the horses were placed in the starting stalls and with a roar from the crowd they were off. It wasn't a very long race, less than a mile and a quarter and as the Newmarket track is very wide the horses were well spread out. The commentator didn't mention She's Our Mare in the early stages and the residents were leaning forward eagerly, trying to establish which was the horse they were supporting. Suddenly the commentator said, 'With a furlong to go, She's Our Mare has burst into the lead,' and the residents started shouting and cheering. It was almost an anti climax when the commentator announced that the winning horse was indeed She's Our Mare.

Vic, Jerry and Glyn were very excited and slapped the Major on the back saying 'well done'. Although he was very pleased, he had to remind them that that was only the first leg of the double and it all depended on the horse called Top Cees, which would be running in two weeks' time. Tricia came to the door, having heard all the shouting and when they explained what had happened she smiled indulgently and said something like 'boys will be boys'.

That evening there was a festive feeling in Hollytree House and Willy said, 'Shall we start planning the party?'

'I'm not sure that's a very good idea,' said the Major. 'We haven't won the double yet, let us wait until after the Cesarewitch.'

He went to bed that night with their congratulations still ringing in his ears and he thought that perhaps living at Hollytree House was going to be a lot better than he originally expected.

Chapter Nine

Life at Hollytree House continued pleasantly, with both staff and residents unaware of the storm clouds which were gathering over it. Jack Smith had been both surprised and excited with the news from Reuben Jones and he decided to set up a meeting with his partner, Ayub Khan. Mr Khan was a quietly spoken man who had a grocer's shop in a town about forty miles away. His mother, now deceased, had opened Hollytree House and the Haven about fifteen years earlier. Mr Khan could not understand how she had acquired someone like Jack Smith as a partner but he gathered it was an arrangement made by her accountant when she was setting up the business and raising the money. She had made a point of speaking to her son only a few months before she had died and made him promise that he would ensure the homes continued as long as there were any residents that needed them.

He and Jack Smith only met quarterly when they looked at the finances of the homes and he left much of the day-to-day management to his partner. He was therefore a bit surprised when Jack telephoned him and asked if they could have a meeting, as they had met less than a month before. They agreed to meet at the Haven on the following Monday.

*

Meanwhile the gentlemen in the liar dice club were taking a much greater interest in horseracing and the Major had to explain that he was not able to look into a crystal ball and find them winners everyday. The ladies of the bridge club had also become much more interested, in addition to planning a party when the second horse won. Due to Jerry's enthusiasm they were all totally convinced that it would. They had also started talking about planning a Millennium party for the end of the year. Tricia, the manager, was quite happy to discuss their plans with them and she thought that a party to celebrate the new century was a very good idea.

One of the differences between her home and most other residential homes was that most of the staff meetings also involved the residents and many plans were made jointly. She believed that if the residents felt they were involved in planning their own lives then it made for a much happier home. After all, as she frequently reminded the staff, they could go home when their shift finished but Hollytree House was home for the residents and it was the staff's job to make the residents as comfortable as possible. Sadly, the same system did not apply at the Haven and Donna ran her home in a very autocratic way. As she regularly told her staff, the residents had to be seen but they did not necessarily have to be heard. The use of medication ensured that this was possible most of the time.

As far as she was concerned, the residents were supposed to do as they were told and to make as little noise as possible. It was not that Donna was a cruel person. When she had first entered residential work she had been enthusiastic and eager to help the residents have a good way of life. However, as she got older she began to feel that her own life was slipping by far too quickly. What she really wanted was to get married and have children of her own. Unfortunately, her only current romantic interest was Denis and he was far from romantic. She was also quite sure that with his drink and drugs problems he would never make a suitable husband. Almost without realising it, her attitude towards the residents had become more autocratic and less caring. The physical condition of the house had also deteriorated from when she originally took over.

On the other hand, Tricia did not see her job as merely accommodating the residents and providing for their basic needs. She believed that every new resident brought in new experiences, ideas and skills and it was the job of herself and her staff to help these residents continue to develop and grow. She did not believe that simply because they were nearing the end of their days life was virtually over.

*

When Jack Smith and Mr Khan arrived at the Haven for their meeting, the house seemed absolutely silent apart from the ever-operating television in the residents' lounge. Donna ushered both Jack Smith and Mr Khan into her office and immediately supplied them with coffee and biscuits. 'Will you want me to sit in on the meeting?' she asked. curious to know what the meeting was about.

'I don't think so,' said Jack, 'but we'll give you a shout if we need you.' And with that he firmly closed the door.

Chapter Ten

Once they had settled down, Mr Khan asked Jack why they were meeting again so soon. Jack replied that he had been thinking about the arrangements and he believed that the two homes could be run more efficiently and profitably if they were separate units rather than operating as a pair. 'After all,' he said, 'it is always possible that one home could finish up subsidising the other.' Mr Khan said gently that he wasn't too worried about making large profits, although as a businessman he obviously preferred to make a profit rather than a loss. He asked Jack Smith if he had any specific suggestions to make because obviously he had called the meeting for a reason.

'Well,' said Jack, 'I have got a number of other interests and I run them very much as sole owner operations. I'm not sure that partnership agreements necessarily suit me.' Mr Khan thought this was very strange as the partnership between Jack and his mother had begun fifteen years ago and this was the first time that Jack Smith had raised any questions about it. He was not a suspicious man but he couldn't help wondering if Jack had an ulterior motive. He asked Jack why he had come to this conclusion after fifteen years and Jack assured him that there was no particular reason apart from wanting to tidy up his own affairs. He said that he wasn't getting any younger and he and his wife had begun to talk about retirement.

Mr Khan then said that if he agreed to split the partnership, which home did Jack suggest went to which owner. Jack Smith replied that he thought he would like to keep the Haven and Mr Khan should have Hollytree House. To say that this surprised Mr Khan had to be an understatement. 'But I have always thought that Hollytree House was by far the nicer home and it is set in much nicer grounds,' replied Mr Khan. He wondered if Jack Smith was suggesting a straight exchange or whether there was to be any cash adjustment. Jack Smith replied that he thought they could look at this together with their accountants but on the whole he was happy to go for a straight exchange. 'After all,' he said, 'I get on very well with the staff here at the Haven and Tricia at Hollytree House always makes me feel a little uncomfortable.' Mr Khan thought that the feelings were probably mutual, as Tricia Beasley and Jack Smith were often at loggerheads about finances. There had been several occasions when Jack had suggested that Tricia spent far too much money on outings and feeding the residents. On reflection he wondered whether this was the motive behind Jack Smith's proposal. 'Perhaps,' he thought, 'that by persuading Donna to cut even more corners, he could make a much more profitable business out of the Haven.'

Jack Smith watched Mr Khan closely and wondered exactly what he was thinking. 'Well,' he said, after a long pause, 'what do you think, Ayub?'

Mr Khan replied that he thought on the face of things it was probably quite a good idea to split the partnership. He very much liked Hollytree House and he thought it was the kind of business he could live comfortably with.

'Well,' said Jack, 'let's shake hands and, subject to a meeting with our accountants, that's what we'll do.'

He then opened the door and to his not very great surprise found Donna lurking in the hall. 'Do come in, Donna,' he said. 'Mr Khan and I have some news for you.'

Mr Khan was rather surprised that Jack was involving Donna so quickly but Jack merely went on to explain that they were thinking of making some changes and it may be that the homes would operate separately in the future. 'I will talk to you more fully,' he said, 'once our plans have been developed, but I assure you that you will not regret the new arrangements.'

With that he and Mr Khan made their farewells and the Haven settled once more into its uneasy torpor. That afternoon Jack Smith telephoned Reuben Jones and told him that he had made the first moves. They arranged to meet on Thursday evening and Reuben Jones said that he would contact James Slighe.

Chapter Eleven

Thursday morning at Hollytree House dawned bright and clear. Paula had arranged to take the residents to see a stately home in the next county. As it happened, only ten residents wanted to go and this included all the gentlemen of the liar dice club and the ladies of the bridge club. They were all able to travel in the minibus and accompanied by Paula and Tim, who was the driver. They set out in high spirits for what seemed to be an interesting day ahead.

They reached the stately home just before 11 o'clock and the first thing they did was to adjourn to the refectory for morning coffee. Paula had arranged for a guide to show them around and they had a most interesting morning. The Major listened to the questions and comments of his fellow residents and thought how nice it was to live with intelligent peers. Once the tour was over they thanked their guide and went back to the refectory for a light lunch. However, just as they were leaving, they noticed that Harriet and Willy were missing.

After a search, some banging and shouting was heard and it transpired that the two ladies had gone into a room they thought led to the toilets. Unfortunately they discovered that they were in a room where cleaning materials were kept and worse still, the handle on the inside had broken off. Apart from a slight loss of face and after they had visited the genuine ladies' toilet, they all clambered aboard the minibus. Jerry kept humming the ditty about two old ladies being locked in the lavatory until Willy complained to Paula, who then very nicely told Jerry to shut up. They were all in good spirits and the Major thought, once again, that there were certainly worse places to live than Hollytree House.

*

That evening Reuben Jones, James Slighe and Jack Smith met in the same pub as on the previous occasion and Reuben asked whether they had thought about his suggestion and what the next step should be. Jack Smith explained that he had had a meeting with Mr Khan and they had provisionally agreed to split the partnership. James Slighe asked whether it would have been easier if Jack had kept Hollytree House. Jack replied that it may have been easier to close the place down but he would then be left without a business. His way would ensure that they acquired Hollytree House at a bargain price and he would still be left with the Haven to run.

'The trouble is,' said James Slighe, 'I know both homes and to be quite frank, it would be easier to make a case for shutting the Haven.'

'Hang on,' said Jack Smith. 'I want to be quite sure that if we go ahead with this plan the Haven will be safe and that you won't be giving me a hard time.'

James Slighe smiled his usual crafty smile and said, 'Of course, Jack, I wouldn't dream of giving you grief over such a wonderful home as the Haven.'

Reuben Jones thought it was about time he intervened and suggested that they got down to the mechanics of the operation. James Slighe said that it was a fairly straightforward operation; he would get his colleagues to find sufficient problems to give them reason to put a closure order on the home. 'The present Director of Social Services is not very bright,' he said, 'and it wouldn't be difficult to pull the wool over his eyes.'

'Right,' said Reuben, 'the first step is for Jack to split the partnership and once that's done you can send your minions in to pull Hollytree House to pieces.'

James Slighe said that it would help if they had a mole on the staff of Hollytree House. Such a person could pass on information and also cause trouble. 'I do know of such a chap,' he said. 'We have co-operated in a previous home and at the present time he is unemployed apart from a bit of work with the Territorial Army.'

Jack Smith said that he could appoint the man as a trainee at Hollytree House, telling Tricia that he wanted him to be prepared for work at the Haven.

'An excellent plan,' said Reuben Jones. 'I will leave you two to sort out the details. In the meantime,' he added, 'I shall tell my client that there may be a possibility of him acquiring Hollytree House. I will, of course, have to swear him to secrecy at this stage, but he is in another branch of our society so it won't be difficult to urge confidentiality.'

At no point in the discussion was there any mention of the residents of Hollytree House or their needs or their future.

Reuben Jones said, 'Then the third step will be for me or Jack or one of my colleagues to approach Mr Khan regarding the sale of his then-defunct business. With any luck we will probably get him to sell us the property for about half a million, which will then leave us with a very nice profit of two and a half million.' He went on to say that he was pretty certain that his property developer friend would be willing to pay three million pounds for the land and he would then demolish Hollytree House. The three conspirators then bade each other good night and went their separate ways.

Chapter Twelve

The following day James Slighe telephoned Jack Smith giving him the name and telephone number of one Ken Pratt. Jack arranged to meet Mr Pratt and after a long discussion decided that he would be very suitable for the task in hand. A few days later Tricia Beasley was surprised when she was approached by Jack Smith, who asked if she would take on a trainee for him. He explained that it was a man he wanted to work ultimately at the Haven but he thought that it would do the man good to have a short spell at Hollytree House. Tricia was a bit suspicious but she agreed to meet Mr Pratt and if she thought he would fit in she would take him on a three-month trial. Jack Smith said he would contact Pratt and get him to call at Hollytree House for an interview.

Excitement was building up in the house as the second leg of the autumn double drew near. Thursday night saw the usual meeting of the liar dice club in the pub. They were all a bit subdued at first because one of the residents, Thomas Healey, known to most as Old Tom, had been found dead in his bed that morning. The Major did not really know Old Tom as he had been unwell and confined to his room ever since the Major had arrived. 'He was a nice old fellow,' said Vic, 'but he didn't mix much.'

'Well he was into his late eighties,' said Jerry. 'I'll probably not mix much when I'm that old.' The others thought this was rather amusing and Glyn said that he could never see the time when Jerry was not mixing and organising no matter how old he was.

They drank their drinks thoughtfully and the talk turned to death in general. Vic said that he wasn't afraid of dying but he worried about where and when. Sitting on the loo, for instance, would be an ignominious way to go. Glyn remarked that he had seen some deaths in the Navy and he thought that he would like to be buried at sea. He said he remembered that somebody had once said that for authentic living it is necessary to have a resolute confrontation of death.

'That was Heidegger,' said Vic, 'a German philosopher who died in the seventies.'

The Major said that he'd seen quite a lot of death during his Army career and he hoped that, like Tom, he would go peacefully in his sleep.

Jerry said, 'For God's sake, lighten up, lads, we're not going to die yet.'

And this led on to a further discussion about God and the possibilities of life afterwards.

Both Vic and the Major were convinced that there was no such thing as Heaven. Glyn said he preferred to keep an open mind. 'There's nothing like a bit of insurance,' he went on.

Jerry then made them all laugh by saying that if there wasn't a Heaven then the various religions had pulled off the biggest advertising scam of all time.

They then had a serious conversation about the merits or otherwise of voluntary euthanasia. They discussed the possibilities of such a practice being abused by unscrupulous relatives. Eventually, however, all four of them agreed that people should be allowed to choose at which point they shuffled off the mortal coil.

The subject then turned to the horse race on the coming Saturday. By now the other three were convinced that the Major was a genius and the result a foregone conclusion. They made their farewells to Les and chatting happily wended their way back to Hollytree House.

Later, in his own room, the Major thought about their discussion regarding God and the existence of Heaven. Although he had always been a sceptic he couldn't help wondering if there was anything in the theory of an afterlife. 'It would be wonderful if I could meet Angela again,' he mused, 'but then on the other hand there are a lot of people I wouldn't want to meet again.' He decided that he had long believed in the writings of such people as Sartre and Kerouac and their theories of existentialism. Over the years he had tried very hard to believe in the existence of a God, but then he always asked himself, which God? Christian, Muslim, Jewish, Hindu, Buddhist. Where did it end? He believed that good and evil existed within every individual and therefore it was a matter of semantics as to whether these two words were converted into God and the Devil. He thought that complete faith must be very comforting as one got older but it wasn't something that he possessed. It's a bit late to change now, old lad, he murmured to himself, as he fell asleep.

CHAPTER THIRTEEN

Friday morning was a bright pleasant day considering it was the end of October. As Tricia drove into the drive of Hollytree House she thought, not for the first time, how much she enjoyed her job and how lucky she was to be working in such a pleasant environment. As she got out of her car she was met by Andy, who was just starting to mow the lawn. 'There's a geezer waiting to see you,' he said. 'A smarmy sort of chap. I'm sure I've seen him before but I can't remember where.'

Tricia thanked Andy and headed for her office. When she entered she saw June chatting to a tall dark-haired man who was wearing a blue tracksuit and brightly coloured trainers. He was holding a cup of coffee and when Tricia entered he did not get up but said, 'Hello there.' June introduced him as Mr Pratt but the man said, 'Everybody calls me Ken.' Tricia was not immediately impressed; the man's smile was too ready and seemed to lack sincerity. She asked him about his previous experience and he was rather vague but said that Mr Smith had his references. He said that he was going to work at the Haven but Mr Smith thought that he could get some training at Hollytree House. He then went on to say that in his opinion he was probably experienced enough but Mr Smith was the boss.

Tricia found Tim and asked him to show Ken Pratt around. Afterwards she asked him if he had any questions but with a smirk he said. 'No thanks, I've got the picture.'

After he had left Tricia rang Donna who told her that she had met Ken Pratt and in her opinion he was quite dishy. This too gave Tricia some cause for disquiet and she then followed up with a telephone call to Jack Smith. She expressed some reluctance but he pressured her saying, 'Look here, we're supposed to co-operate with each other and it's not a lot to ask. After all,' he went on, 'you're experienced enough to make something of Mr Pratt and Donna needs more help at the Haven.' After some further discussion she agreed to take the man on a three-month trial. Jack Smith said he would contact Pratt and tell him to report to Tricia on the 1st of November.

*

After dinner on Friday evening all the talk in the sitting room was about tomorrow's race. By now most of the residents were very interested and Willy and her lady friends were planning the celebration party for tomorrow evening. They had persuaded Tim to go to the local wine merchants on Saturday morning. 'Supposing we don't win?' said Vic. 'Who's going to pay for the wine?'

The ladies replied that they would pay for it initially and the men could refund them out of their winnings.

'Jerry has told us that it's a certainty so there will be no problem about the money,' said Willy. They were also planning to do some special cooking with the help of Mrs Burton and Mrs Halliday, the two cooks.

The Major went to bed that night fervently hoping that his selection wasn't going to let everyone down. *They will probably send me to Coventry or worse still, back to the Haven.*

With that unhappy thought he fell asleep.

CHAPTER FOURTEEN

On Saturday morning there was an air of high expectancy during breakfast, everybody was talking much more than usual. Tricia, who was on duty, thought to herself, 'Well I've never been much in favour of gambling but if it makes them so enthusiastic and interested it could be a good thing.' On the other hand she thought, 'If the wretched horse loses then this evening could be a very despondent affair.' She need not have worried on that score because at three o'clock that afternoon all the residents and the staff who were on duty gathered round the television. The race was nearly twice as long as the previous one and at one point their horse seemed to be well in the rear. However, about half a mile from home it advanced towards the front of the pack and the residents shouted their horse home. The men all slapped the Major on the back and congratulated him and several of the ladies actually gave him a kiss. All the Major could do was breathe a fervent 'thank you' to Lady Luck.

That evening the party was a great success. Tim and Andy had taken up the carpet in the dining room and Tim provided an impromptu disco. Most of the ladies danced and most of the men sat around the edges of the floor, drinking. The Major thought, 'It's just like when we were adolescents, the girls enjoying themselves and the boys wishing they had the nerve to join in.'

The one exception was Vic, who spent most of the evening

dancing and much of it with Poppy. 'Hey up lads,' said Jerry to Glyn and the Major. 'It looks as if Vic has designs on Poppy.' Poppy was the youngest of the four bridge ladies and although she was in her early seventies she was still a very attractive woman. That night she was dressed in a powder blue dress and seemed to float as she danced. 'Oh you know our Vic,' said Glyn grumpily, 'any port in a storm.'

At about nine o'clock they broke off to enjoy the excellent food and drink which the ladies had provided. The mood was tempered slightly when Jerry proposed a toast to absent friends and they all thought it was such a pity that Tom could not have enjoyed the evening with them. Time seemed to fly by and when Tricia announced that it was eleven-thirty most of the residents were surprised but started to reluctantly drift off to bed.

Willy threw her arms around the Major and said, 'Thank you for a wonderful evening.' The Major blushed and replied that he thought everybody had contributed. 'Yes,' she acknowledged, 'but it would not have been possible without you providing us with the reason to celebrate.'

Sunday was something of an anti climax; it was quite clear that some of the residents were experiencing mild hangovers and breakfast was a rather subdued affair. After lunch Tricia called a meeting and explained that Tom's funeral was to be held on the coming Thursday. She said there was no reason for delay as the death was due to natural causes and something which she and the doctor had been expecting.

She asked how many residents would like to go to the funeral, although she explained that it was actually to be a cremation as Tom had requested. To her surprise all but two of the residents wanted to go, the exceptions were the oldest resident, Mrs Hargreaves, who was ninety-five and very frail and Mrs Robertson, known to everybody as Robbie, who said she would stay and keep Mrs Hargreaves company.

Jerry suggested that they should buy lots of flowers out of their winnings to make sure that Tom got a good send off. Everybody thought that this was a good idea and Harriet and Willy volunteered to go to a florist in the town and arrange this. Glyn, however, said that he thought that spending too much money on flowers would be a bit wasteful, especially in view of the fact that Tom was to be cremated. He suggested that they decide on a sum of money and split it between flowers and a donation to the local hospice. Everybody agreed that this was a good idea.

The liar dice group were obviously depressed at the talk of funerals and started what amounted to a philosophical discussion. Jerry said, 'The world we live in now has changed beyond all recognition, there seems to be no respect for other people.'

Glyn added, 'It's much nearer the law of the jungle, every man for himself.'

Vic's opinion was that there were too many parasites eager to feather their own nests regardless of anyone else and the Major agreed. 'In my opinion,' he said, 'it starts at the top from the Prime Minister through to almost all politicians. They will tell you that they are in it "to make a difference". What they really mean is to make a difference to their own lives. They think it will give them power and prestige, not to mention money.'

Jerry scratched his head and said, 'Yes but it doesn't stop there. People used to say that estate agents and journalists were the worse parasites but who would you nominate?'

'Anyone in the legal system,' said Vic. 'Solicitors and barristers who are prepared to defend people they know to be guilty and judges who put their own personal opinions before logic and justice. They live their lives cocooned from the real world.'

Glyn's nomination was union leaders. 'They make lots of

noise, talk about strikes and industrial action and yet continue to draw decent salaries and expenses while their members often lose their jobs.'

The Major said, 'I still think politicians are the worst people of all, they can introduce laws and impose taxes knowing that they can find loopholes for themselves and award themselves higher salaries and expense allowances.'

Jerry then said, 'Lets face it, chaps, we live in a society which we no longer understand and which has neither time nor space for people like us.'

On that depressing note they lapsed into silence and each sat thinking their own thoughts.

Chapter Fifteen

Thursday morning was a sombre affair in Hollytree House; all the residents were very quiet over breakfast and then at ten-thirty they had coffee and assembled in the hall. Most of the ladies had decided to dress themselves in black or dark clothing and all the men were wearing black ties. Just before eleven they all struggled on board the minibus and those who could not fit on the minibus climbed into Tricia's car. When they got to the crematorium they were met by Mr Khan, who went round shaking hands with everybody and conveying his sympathy for their loss.

The only other person there was a tall, pale young man whom Tricia introduced as Tom's nephew. He and his mother, Tom's sister, lived in Kent but she was not well enough to travel so Michael, the nephew, was the only family representative. Jerry said very quietly, 'Not much of a send-off then, a bunch of old codgers and one relative.'

The service was brief and uninspiring and when Tricia asked the nephew if he would like to come back to Hollytree House for lunch he hastily declined. He explained that he had to go to a meeting but would come back sometime next week to tidy up his uncle's affairs. Later over lunch Jerry continued the theme of how few of them had relatives who cared whether they were alive or not. Glyn remarked that as long as they had friends there was no need to be lonely and they didn't need their relatives.

'Nevertheless,' said Vic, 'it's not right the way old people are shunted into homes and then forgotten. Look at Mrs Hargreaves for example, she has a number of relatives who live nearby and what do they do? They come and see her for about half an hour just before Christmas.' The general consensus was that very few families nowadays were prepared to take care of their elderly relatives.

Jerry said, 'It seems almost a crime to be old and still hanging around.'

That evening the liar dice club did not go on their usual trip to the pub, they thought that as a mark of respect they ought to give it a miss. Instead they sat quietly in the lounge and Jerry played the piano, leaving the music room door open. It wasn't long before some of the residents started to join in and sing and the Major was interested to see how a pleasant musical evening could evolve out of what had been a very sad day. He came to the conclusion that because many old people become philosophical about death, grief is not so overwhelming.

He noticed that Vic and Poppy were sitting side by side on the settee and at one point looked to be holding hands. Jerry stopped playing when the supper drinks arrived and came over to sit by the Major. 'Vic and Poppy are getting on very well,' he remarked. 'Mind you,' he went on, 'you couldn't describe Vic as a fast worker. Poppy came to live here nearly a year ago, and I know he's fancied her all that time.'

'Well they seem very happy,' replied the Major, 'and it's never too late for love.'

Chapter Sixteen

While the residents were quietly enjoying themselves another meeting was taking place across town which was much more sinister. The consortium of three had gathered to start discussing the next phase of their unpleasant plan. Jack Smith reported that he had arranged for Ken Pratt to start at Hollytree House and Reuben Jones asked James Slighe to give them some idea about the next steps.

Slighe explained that there were actually three prongs to the attack: first of all he would start sending his staff in to find sufficient faults for him to issue notices; secondly he would liaise with Ken Pratt to create situations which could be used in the reporting procedure; thirdly he and his staff would start a campaign of minor harassment, visiting the home unannounced before breakfast or at suppertime when their visits would create maximum disturbance. They would also telephone staff in their own homes to see whether they could create alarm and unrest.

Reuben Jones said that it sounded as if James Slighe had done this before. Slighe smiled and said 'Oh yes, I like to see the look on the manager's or proprietor's faces when they realise that they are about to lose their livelihood. 'But what about the residents,' asked Reuben, 'do you take their needs and feelings into account?'

'Not my problem,' replied Slighe. 'In any case one place is much the same as the next and when they do move most of them are barely aware of the difference.' He went on, 'Mind you I've never done it for money before so this will be a bit of a novelty and we will have to ensure that it is done very carefully and with complete confidentiality.'

Jack Smith wanted to be reassured that whatever went on at Hollytree House would not have repercussions on the Haven. Slighe assured him, as he had done on a previous occasion, that he would make sure the two homes were considered quite separately. Reuben Jones pointed out that Jack Smith would have to complete the transfers of the Haven to himself and Hollytree House to Mr Khan. Smith replied that both their accountants and the solicitors were in the process of drawing up the final agreements and certainly by the end of November the separation should have taken place.

Once again there was absolutely no mention of the welfare of the residents or the future of the staff involved.

Jack Smith did raise the question of Ken Pratt and asked whether Slighe would agree that he could continue to be employed at the Haven once Hollytree House closed down. Slighe assured him that that would be no problem because he had no intention of losing touch with Pratt, who could be very useful but could also be dangerous if he was not kept on a tight rein. He explained that none of his other staff would be aware that Pratt was working for him and indeed none of his other staff would be remotely aware of the motivation behind their actions.

'It is important that my staff believe that their actions are genuine.'

'It sounds as if you treat your staff like mushrooms,' said Jack Smith. 'Keep them in the dark and cover them in bullshit.'

Slighe laughed and said, 'Yes, something like that.'

Reuben Jones said that he thought everything seemed to be very satisfactory and he would continue to keep up a quiet dialogue with his client, the property developer. Once again they made their farewells and left James Slighe to open his unpleasant and unscrupulous campaign.

Chapter Seventeen

On Monday the 1st of November Ken Pratt joined the staff team at Hollytree House. He arrived promptly at eight o'clock still clad in his blue tracksuit and spent the morning creating a very good impression with the ladies. The men however were not so enthusiastic. 'The bugger's too smooth by far,' said Glyn. Tricia held a meeting with him just before coffee time and stressed that the main purpose in Hollytree House was to provide the residents with a good quality of life and that she felt it was important that every resident was treated as an individual. Pratt replied that he hadn't got any problems with that because he had aged parents of his own. He said that he knew exactly what old people needed, smirking rather unpleasantly.

At coffee time he was introduced to Andy, the gardener, who said, 'Haven't we met before?'

'Of course,' replied Pratt, 'we met when I came for the interview.'

'I'm sure that we met before that,' said Andy, but Pratt replied that he really didn't think so. Andy continued to rack his brains. During the afternoon the Major went up to his room and was surprised to see that a number of his possessions had been moved. Being ex army he was a very methodical man, almost to the point of obsessiveness, keeping everything in its place. Whilst they were having their cup of afternoon tea he mentioned the disturbance to Glyn and Jerry.

'That's odd,' said Glyn, 'I was sure someone had been in my room.' And Jerry agreed that he too was somewhat puzzled.

They decided that it must have happened during the lunch period and the only person who was not present at lunch was the new man, Ken Pratt. Glyn asked whether they should report the incident to Tricia but they agreed that really there was very little they could say at the moment because nothing was missing. They resolved, however, to keep an eye on Mr Pratt. After dinner the same day Mrs Hargreaves had one of her turns and the staff had to take her back to her room. Because she was so elderly her bedroom was on the ground floor and it was simply a case of putting her in a wheelchair. The other residents were quite worried because she was very much a favourite of theirs and they were conscious of the fact that they had quite recently lost old Tom. 'I do hope she's going to be alright,' said Willy and the other ladies also expressed concern.

That evening Andy was watching a wild life programme on the television when he suddenly remembered where he had encountered Pratt before. Two years previously he had been asked to quote for some work at a country house just outside town. As he went up the drive he saw another man leaving in a rather battered pickup. The drive wasn't quite wide enough so Andy pulled over and allowed the other vehicle to creep past. He expected the other man to smile an acknowledgement but instead received a rather unpleasant scowl.

When he got to the house he found the elderly lady owner rather distressed. She explained that she wanted the patio area repaired and some other work including a tree being cut down in the garden. She had asked Andy how much it would cost and after some simple calculations he told her that he could do the work for about eight hundred pounds. She was very relieved and explained that the man who had just left had quoted over three thousand pounds and had become very unpleasant when she said that she thought that was too much. Andy remembered that the man was Ken Pratt and decided to have a quiet word with Tricia the next time he saw her.

CHAPTER EIGHTEEN

A few days later the usually quiet and pleasant breakfast time in Hollytree House was disturbed by the visit of two women. They introduced themselves as Mrs Phillips and Miss Burley and told Paula that they were inspectors making an unannounced visit. Paula told them that the manager, Tricia Beasley, was on a few days holiday.

'Yes we know,' said one.

But the other one hastily interrupted and said, 'Oh that's just a coincidence as we work to a pre-arranged timetable.'

Mrs Phillips said that she would like to look through some of the records, starting with the staff rota and then moving on to the medication records and the menu book. Miss Burley said that in the meantime she would start having a look round the premises. Paula said that the residents were having their breakfast and she did hope that they weren't going to be disturbed. She was assured that they would be as discreet as possible and really there was no need for the residents to be aware as to whom they were. Paula replied that she was afraid many of the residents would want to know who any strange visitors were and that the current group of residents were very bright people.

She left one inspector in the office looking through the records and accompanied Miss Burley around the house. They went into the dining room first and Paula explained to the residents that she was accompanied by a lady from Social

Services who just wanted to look around. When they went into the music room the woman looked at the fireplace in which was set an arrangement of twigs and flowers.

'Why is there no fireguard around that fire?' she asked.

Paula explained that they never used the fireplace, the central heating was quite sufficient and that was why they had the floral arrangement instead of a fireguard.

The woman said, 'You are aware that all fireplaces should have suitable fireguards,' and Paula thought this was very strange in view of her explanation.

Meanwhile in the dining room a discussion was taking place; the Major asked Tim who these women were and why they were coming round so early in the morning.

Jerry said, 'Oh they're a collection of do-gooders who work for the local authority.'

Glyn added, 'Yes, they're a pain in the ass.'

Vic said, 'Oh be fair, that doesn't apply to all social workers, I used to teach philosophy to groups of trainee social workers and I'd say that about fifty per cent of them are good people who are genuinely seeking to help others. Twenty five per cent of the rest seem to come into social work because they have problems of their own and the remainder are looking for power.' He went on: 'It's the last group that are the most dangerous; they are often the least intelligent and useless at everything they've attempted but they feel they have a right to tell other people how to lead their lives.'

In the meantime Paula was getting more and more uneasy about the way the inspector she accompanied was making notes and seemed to be nit picking about trivial items. She wanted to know why the cook appeared to be having her breakfast in the kitchen and Paula explained that she obviously had to wait until everyone else had had their breakfast.

'Nevertheless,' the woman said, 'staff should eat at the staff table.'

They eventually went back to the office and found that the other inspector had completed her examination of the documents.

'Everything was alright, I hope?' said Paula.

'Well that depends by what you mean alright,' was the reply. 'I found a number of gaps and you will be receiving a full report of our visit.'

Paula showed them out and unusually for her felt very uneasy. There was something about their manner which was different from previous inspections.

Chapter Nineteen

When Tricia got back from her holiday – she had been walking in Wales – she was faced by two worried people. Paula told her about the inspection and how uneasy she'd felt by the attitude of the two inspectors. Tricia tried to reassure her and said, 'It was probably just a one off, but in any case there's no point in worrying until we get the report.' After she had seen Paula, Andy asked if she could spare him a few minutes. He told her about his disquiet regarding Ken Pratt and Tricia replied that she was not at all surprised. She went on to say that as long as Pratt kept his nose clean at Hollytree House he would be moving on to the Haven early in the New Year. Andy was not reassured by Tricia's comments regarding Pratt and resolved to keep a close eye on him.

In the afternoon Jerry challenged the Major to a game of chess. They were fairly well matched and after they had won one game each they sat chatting in the music room. Jerry told him that his wife had died several years ago and before that she had been ill for a long time with multiple sclerosis. The Major sympathised and said that perhaps he had been lucky in that his wife had enjoyed good health until the day she died. Jerry went on to tell him that Vic, too, had had a very difficult time as his wife had developed Alzheimer's disease in her late fifties and died when she was only sixty-three.

'That's the trouble with growing old,' the Major said. 'Everybody has a fund of depressing stories.'

'Let's change the subject then,' said Jerry. 'How do you get on with Bridie?'

'How do you mean "get on?"' asked the Major. 'She's always very pleasant and I certainly haven't got any complaints.'

'Ah yes,' said Jerry, 'but have you discovered her expertise in the bath?'

'I haven't the faintest idea what you're talking about,' said the Major. 'I certainly haven't had anyone assist me in my bath, kindly explain.'

Jerry replied that a few months earlier he had hurt his back and had great difficulty getting in and out of the bath. Tim was away so Jerry had asked Bridie if she would mind giving him a hand. 'Then she offered to wash my back,' said Jerry, 'and before long she was giving me a very helpful massage. Glyn also avails himself of her services and we give her twenty or thirty pounds a time. She is apparently saving very hard to take herself and her two sons back to Ireland to get away from her husband. By all accounts he's a drunk and a bully and she needs to go back to her family so that the boys can grow up in peace.'

The Major thought for a moment and then said, 'Well it seems a bit unusual to me.'

'Oh come on,' replied Jerry, 'when you're our age a bit of a feminine kindness can be very welcome. She always makes it very light-hearted and says that it's not that much different from bathing her own boys. Vic, of course, used to join in but now he's involved with Poppy he's given up and I'm sure Bridie would be glad of the extra money.'

'Well,' said the Major, 'I would be quite happy to help her out financially but I'm not at all sure that I could be so bold, I really will have to think about it.'

At that moment the tea bell sounded and with some relief he led the way into the sitting room.

Chapter Twenty

The month of November was in direct contrast to the very pleasant preceding month. It was mostly grey, cold and wet and the weather seemed to affect everyone's mood. On several occasions the men found Ken Pratt snooping in their rooms and they decided to raise the issue at the next joint meeting. After Tricia had opened the meeting Jerry asked her whether, apart from Lucy, who did the cleaning, there was any need for other staff to go into their rooms. Tricia replied that all the residents had keys of their own and staff should only go into their rooms if they were invited to do so. However she pointed out that there were occasional exceptions to this: if for instance someone was ill or if any maintenance was needed.

The Major thought that the discussion was a bit vague so he said that he knew Ken Pratt went into their rooms without invitation. Pratt responded with saying that he only did so to check if there were any maintenance problems and Tricia said with some surprise that that was Tim's responsibility. The meeting agreed that the residents' rooms were private and staff should not enter without permission.

They then went on to discuss other matters including plans for Christmas, which was fast approaching. The discussion was lively and there was much enthusiasm for Christmas plans and the Millennium party. The atmosphere became much more light-hearted but the Major was aware of Pratt glaring at him malevolently. After dinner, as he was going up to his room, the Major met Pratt at the top of the stairs. 'You should be careful on the stairs,' said Pratt. 'Old people have been known to kill themselves falling downstairs.'

The Major could tell by the look on Pratt's face that this wasn't just a light-hearted remark. 'Don't worry,' he said, 'I will be very careful.'

Later, when they were playing liar dice, he told the other men about the encounter.

Jerry said, 'Yes I think our Mr Pratt is a nasty piece of work and we all need to look out for each other.'

Vic wondered just what motive Pratt had for going in their rooms and whether he also went into the ladies' rooms.

Glyn, who was still a big strong man despite his seventy-eight years said, 'Well I hope he isn't stupid enough to threaten me because he might just be unlucky.'

They continued their game and shortly afterwards the supper drinks came in and the Major dismissed the matter from his mind. Nevertheless it did just cast a bit of a cloud onto what had recently been a much happier way of life. That night he couldn't settle and lay tossing and turning until at last he fell into an uneasy sleep.

CHAPTER TWENTY-ONE

Towards the end of the month at about eight-thirty on a very dark, wet night there was a thunderous knocking on the door. Tricia went to open it and was faced by a man with a face as unpleasant as the weather. 'We have been standing out here for ages,' he said. 'Aren't you supposed to have a working bell?'

She realised that the man was James Slighe and he was accompanied by Mrs Phillips. 'I'm very sorry,' she replied, 'but it did work earlier today.'

'Well,' he said, 'we've come on an unannounced inspection.'

'Another one?' queried Tricia. 'Surely there was one less than a month ago when I was on holiday?'

'We are entitled to make as many as we like if we are unhappy about a home and our last inspection was far from satisfactory.'

Tricia replied that she had not seen a report of the last visit and Slighe said, 'Don't worry, you will soon. Now we would like to take a look round please.'

They left their outdoor clothes in the office and Tricia started to show them round.

'Who else is on duty?' Slighe asked.

Tricia explained that June was in the kitchen preparing the supper drinks and Edna was upstairs helping one of the older ladies to prepare for bed. 'Most of our residents are very able,' she explained, 'and are well capable of looking after themselves.'

Slighe muttered something to Mrs Phillips and she went off upstairs while Slighe accompanied Tricia into the sitting room.

Again the residents were surprised to see a stranger, particularly at that time of the night, and Tricia reluctantly introduced him.

Slighe said, in a very patronising manner, that he did not wish to disturb them but he and his colleague were simply making sure that they were being properly looked after. Jerry spoke up and said that they were very well looked after, thank you very much. The Major asked if it wouldn't be more polite to come along during the day and by appointment. James Slighe actually flushed and said, 'I'm just doing my job,' and asked Tricia if they could move on.

In the music room he asked why there wasn't a fireguard. Paula had forgotten to mention that an inspector on a previous visit had raised it and Tricia explained that they never used the fire. 'Nevertheless,' said Slighe, 'there should not only be a fireguard but it must be screwed to the fireplace.' Tricia found these comments totally bewildering.

Just outside the dining room was a small conservatory, it was a real suntrap and some of the older residents would sit in there often having a quiet nap.

James Slighe opened the door and said, 'This looks dangerous.'

Tricia looked puzzled and said, 'What do you mean?'

'Well it's nearly all glass,' Slighe replied.

'Yes, well, conservatories are mostly all glass,' Tricia replied, looking slightly bemused.

'Well, suppose a resident fell through?' Slighe rejoined.

'But it is strong double-glazed glass,' Tricia protested.

'Nevertheless,' said Slighe, 'it must not be used in the

future and I have no time to argue. This room must be out of bounds to residents.'

In the kitchen June was surprised and flustered when they appeared and in her embarrassment spilled some water out of the kettle onto the floor. Slighe asked Tricia if the staff were aware of health and safety procedures and she replied that of course they were. He then asked why there was no cook on duty and she explained that one cook did breakfast and lunch and the other did tea and dinner.

'Well, I'm not happy about inexperienced people in the kitchen,' Slighe said.

Tricia almost lost her temper. 'For goodness sake, Mr Slighe, June is a wife and mother and obviously very experienced in a kitchen.'

Just then Mrs Phillips came into the kitchen and said everything was in order upstairs but there were no loo rolls in the men's toilets. Tricia was surprised to hear this and made a mental note to check later.

They went back into the office and Slighe said that he was not at all happy with certain aspects of the home. 'For one thing,' he said, 'when we ask that something should be done we expect it to be done, not just ignored.' Tricia wasn't at all sure what he was referring to but suspected that he was still going on about the fireguard.

As they were putting on their coats Slighe said, 'You will be receiving our report in the very near future.'

After Tricia had shown them out she checked the bell and was surprised to see that the battery was missing. 'That's very strange,' she thought. She then decided to ring Donna at the Haven and was not surprised to hear that at exactly eight-thirty they too had had a visit.

Chapter Twenty-Two

The following morning Tricia rang Mr Khan and told him about the inspector's visit. Mr Khan thought it was unusual that they should have had two visits in less than a month but said that he would contact Jack Smith. When he did so Smith told him that the Haven too had had visits but there was no need to worry; he suspected that the Social Services Department had probably heard rumours of the two homes being separated. After his conversation with Mr Khan, Smith put the phone down, smiling to himself. He then made a call to James Slighe who told him that progress had been made at Hollytree House and that he should ignore the Haven inspection, as it was just a smoke screen.

He then asked Smith how the transfer was going and Smith told him that all the formalities would be completed on the 10th of December. Slighe reminded him to inform the authorities officially of the ownership changes because that would give them an excuse for another inspection before Christmas.

Meanwhile Paula had arranged a theatre outing for the residents. They were going to see a play by Dylan Thomas called *Under Milkwood*. Jerry, who was very well read, said that it was set in a village call Llareggub, which was Thomas's idea of a joke as it did, of course, mean bugger all backwards and was very unkind about the villagers.

Only ten of the residents wanted to go, as for some of the older ones it would be a rather late outing. Vic and Poppy were now making no secret of their budding relationship even to the extent of holding hands in the theatre. Most people were quite happy with this and only Glyn and Jerry were critical, the latter saying, 'The poor old bugger's going soft in the head.' The evening was extremely enjoyable and although it was almost eleven o'clock before they got back from the theatre most of the residents were not ready to end the day. Instead they opted for a cup of cocoa and continued chatting in the sitting room until almost midnight. Tim was on sleeping-in duty and didn't mind staying up late, as the residents were so happy.

Mrs Hargreaves' health was deteriorating and on the 7th of December she was transferred to hospital as she was suffering from pneumonia. All the residents were very concerned and Harriet and Willy arranged a visiting rota.

*

Three days later Jack Smith and Ayub Khan met with their solicitors and accountants and the transfer was completed. Jack Smith wished his former partner every success and after the meeting telephoned both Reuben Jones and James Slighe with the good news. Slighe told Smith that it would be better if he didn't call him at the office for the next few weeks and gave him his mobile number. He reminded him to let the authority know of the change and said that all he had to do was keep his head down. Smith replied that he was happy to do that but in turn reminded Slighe that he expected the Haven to be left alone. 'After all,' he added, 'you wouldn't want your bosses to know of our arrangement, would you?' And chuckling quietly, he put down the telephone.

Chapter Twenty-Three

On Wednesday morning the weather was very pleasant and as Harriet and Willy were going to visit Mrs Hargreaves in the afternoon, Joyce and Poppy decided they would go to do some Christmas shopping. Paula said that she would take them into town after she had dropped Harriet and Willy at the hospital. After lunch they set off and when she left Joyce and Poppy they said that in addition to doing some shopping they would have a cup of tea at Poppy's favourite café and Paula arranged to meet them again in two hours.

She then went back to the hospital to meet up with Harriet and Willy and all three of them sat around Mrs Hargreaves' bed chatting happily. Mrs Hargreaves was obviously glad to see them but she was clearly very frail and didn't have a lot to say. However, as Harriet and Willy were never at a loss for words the afternoon passed very quickly. Just after four o'clock they made their farewells, promising someone would be coming to visit Mrs Hargreaves the following day. Paula drove into town and although Joyce and Poppy were at the agreed meeting place they were in a somewhat distressed state.

They had spent the first hour happily shopping and then went for a very pleasant cup of tea and a mince pie. Unfortunately at about three-thirty the town centre suddenly seemed full of school children and Joyce and Poppy decided to go into a department store. The entrance they chose was blocked by a crowd of boys around fourteen or fifteen years of age. They made no attempt to move and Joyce said, 'Excuse me, boys, may we get into the store?'

At first they seemed to take absolutely no notice until one turned round and said, 'Fuck off, you old bag, use another door.'

Poppy was outraged and said, 'You can't speak to us like that.'

'Oh yes we can,' was the retort, 'now clear off.' And one actually pushed Poppy out of the way.

Joyce clutched her friend's arm and said, 'Come on Poppy, we'll go further up.'

'Oh Poppy,' cried one boy. 'The old bag thinks she's a flower.'

And another boy said, 'Why don't you wrinklies get lost.'

A middle-aged man who was passing remonstrated with the boys but got an equally rude response. At that point a security guard from the store who had been alerted by a customer came out and made the boys disperse.

Both ladies were very upset and discontinued any thought of further shopping and made their way back to where they were to meet Paula. When Paula and the other two heard their story they were very indignant. When they got back to Hollytree House Tricia was told of the incident and she asked if they could identify the school to which the boys belonged by their uniforms. Joyce was able to do this and Tricia said that it was a bit late now but she would ring the school the following morning.

The other residents were all very upset on behalf of Poppy and Joyce and Vic in particular said, 'You're not to go out again without me.' They then went on to talk about the lack of respect for the elderly in modern society. Glyn remarked that grandparents used to be respected but not any more.

Jerry said that behaviour seemed to be deteriorating throughout society as a whole. 'There is more yobbish behaviour, more vandalism and more bullying than ever before,' he said. One significant problem is that most children have absolutely no respect for their teachers and probably very little respect for their parents.

The general consensus was that unpleasant behaviour was now the norm rather than the exception. The incident threw a pall over the evening and Joyce and Poppy went up to bed immediately after the supper drink.

Chapter Twenty-Four

The following morning, however, Tricia had something else to worry about. She received a letter from Mr Khan telling her that he was now the sole owner of Hollytree House and when she rang Donna she in turn confirmed that Jack Smith was now the sole owner of the Haven. Tricia was a little puzzled because Smith had apparently emphasised to Donna that in future the two homes were not to be involved with each other. While Tricia was worrying about this Paula came in and said that there was a car parked at the bottom of the drive and it looked to her as if they were Social Services inspectors.

Tricia asked Tim if he would be kind enough to walk down the drive and ask what it was they wanted. He came back saying that they had looked a little confused but told him that they were simply checking who was coming on duty. They said that there were discrepancies in the staff rota. Tricia was furious; she was quite certain that there were no discrepancies in the staff rota, and she was about to go storming down the drive when Andy reported that the car had now gone.

She called an impromptu staff meeting without the residents. Apart from her and Paula there was Tim, Andy, Bridie and Lucy, the cleaner, present. She explained that she had had this letter from Mr Khan telling her that he was now the sole owner.

'Well, we certainly won't miss Smarmy Smith,' said Tim with a wry smile.

A MAJOR MIRACLE

Tricia then went on to say that the Home seemed to be under some pressure from the Social Services and although it may simply be because of the change of ownership they should all be very careful, they should continue to work in their usual caring and competent manner.

After the meeting she decided to ring the school regarding the incident on the previous day, and after some delay was eventually put through to the Head teacher. She explained the problem but the Head was very brusque and said, 'In the first instance you're not sure it was boys from my school and in any case we can't be held responsible for what children do after school.' After a few more heated words Tricia said rather unwisely that if that was his attitude towards the elderly it was no wonder that the children attending his school were so badly behaved. The Head was furious and said he would refer the matter to the LEA.

Less than half an hour later the telephone rang and Paula, who was sitting in the office, answered it. She went looking for Tricia and said, 'I'm afraid there's a rather pompous unpleasant man on the telephone asking for you.'

When Tricia answered the telephone the man introduced himself as Derek Longbottom and said he was a school's advisor. He then went on to say that Tricia should not ring up schools making unproven allegations. Tricia tried to be reasonable and explained that she was simply worried about the welfare of her residents. The man replied rudely that he had better things to do than waste his time arguing with somebody who ran a small residential home and in future would she kindly go through the proper channels or better still, not interfere in local authority business. 'You may be aware,' he said, 'that I am a former teacher myself and we teachers regard ourselves as academics not child minders.'

Tricia was upset by these ridiculous and somewhat pathetic comments but she spoke to the residents whilst they were having their afternoon cup of tea and apologised for the fact that she had made little progress. She suggested that in future residents went into the town centre during school hours. Most of the men were up in arms about this and Vic said, 'It comes to something when we cannot walk freely in our own town.' Discussions were still going on at suppertime and the Major went to bed thinking that present day society made growing old seem more like a crime.

Chapter Twenty-Five

The pressure on Tricia continued the following morning when James Slighe telephoned to say that he had had complaints from a colleague in the LEA to the effect that she had been trying to cause trouble for one of the local schools. She tried to explain that she was merely concerned for the welfare of her residents but he brushed her explanation aside and said that he was getting very worried about her attitude and the problems at Hollytree House. He said that he had been informed that Mr Khan was now the sole owner and he was going to contact him regarding his disquiet.

Tricia put the telephone down and stared out of the window; it was raining hard and the visibility was poor, not that that registered with Tricia who saw nothing because she was lost in a world suddenly set in turmoil. She thought back to just a few weeks earlier when everything seemed so pleasant and she was really enjoying her job. She thought that she would have to go home that evening and discuss the matter with her husband. He was a very caring man who had done quite a lot of work at Hollytree House and who was almost as concerned for the residents as she was.

Meanwhile Paula and Tim had put their heads together and during the coffee break they suggested to the residents that they would organise a Christmas shopping expedition in a small pleasant market town, which was about twenty miles away. They said they could have lunch out and make a really interesting day of it. The residents were very pleased and thought it was an excellent idea, although Vic commented again that it was a pity that elderly people could be driven out of the town where many of them had grown up.

Jerry said, 'If only these kids realised that they too will be old one day.' He went on to say, 'If only we could put old heads on young shoulders.'

Harriet said, 'The truth of the matter is that the whole of society seems to be reverting to the law of the jungle; a bit like dog eat dog, everybody is so busy looking after themselves and perhaps their immediate family, they have no interest in the plight of others.'

'Oh that's a bit sweeping,' said Joyce, 'look at the staff here, they care about us.'

'Alright,' said Harriet, 'I admit that there are exceptions to every rule.'

The Major thought the discussion was becoming very depressing and he decided to go into the garden and look for Andy. On two afternoons a week the Major had got into the habit of visiting the small brick shed at the bottom of the garden where Andy kept his mowers and other tools. Quite often he would persuade one of the cooks to give him a flask of coffee, which he would then take down to the shed and share with Andy. They had some fascinating discussions; the Major would talk about his army life and Andy would tell him of the interesting range of jobs which he had held since leaving agricultural college. On one occasion the Major mentioned his disquiet about the behaviour of Ken Pratt. Andy sympathised and said that he too was not at all impressed by Pratt. Unknown to both of them Pratt had several times observed the Major going down to the shed and made a mental note for future reference.

Chapter Twenty-Six

On Friday morning Tricia received a letter from James Slighe; in it he wrote that as there had been changes in ownership there would be an announced inspection on the 21st of December. Tricia thought that this was most inconvenient as it was so near to Christmas. She rang Donna to ask whether she too had had a letter, Donna said no and reminded Tricia that Jack Smith had said they were no longer to be involved together. Tricia then called a meeting for both staff and residents and informed them that there was to be an inspection on the 21st.

Some of the staff were alarmed and the residents were clearly unhappy that disruption would take place so near to Christmas. 'After all,' said Jerry, 'its supposed to be the time of goodwill and merriment and from what I've seen of those inspectors there won't be much of either.' Tricia tried to soothe everybody's anxieties by assuring them that Hollytree House was a good home and there would be nothing to worry about.

After lunch the Major knocked on the office door because he wanted to talk to Tricia about Christmas plans. Although he knocked twice, when he opened the door he found her sitting with her head in her hands and looking very near to tears. He hastily said that he didn't want to presume or interfere but was there anything he could do. 'My wife used to say a problem shared could be a problem halved,' he said. Tricia replied that he was very kind but she really wasn't sure that there was anything he could do. The problem seemed to be linked with the splitting up of the two homes.

'A good thing, if you ask me,' said the Major. 'The two homes are like chalk and cheese and it seems strange that it is our home that seems to be under pressure from the Social Services.' Tricia explained that she had asked Mr Khan to call in that evening so that they could discuss the matter. The Major asked if she would mind if he talked to his friends. 'Oh no,' said Tricia, 'they have a right to know but I would be glad if the older and frailer residents were not alarmed.' The Major promised that he would be very discreet.

Ayub Khan called during dinner and afterwards took some time to talk to the residents in the sitting room. He asked them about their plans for Christmas and the New Year and assured them that if there was anything he could do to help, they only had to ask. He said that he would give Tricia one thousand pounds towards Christmas and the Millennium party and Vic thanked him on behalf of the residents. Mr Khan could tell from their smiles that they were very pleased.

Afterwards Mr Khan and Tricia had a discussion in her office. He was equally puzzled as to the reasons for the increased pressure and wondered if Jack Smith was somehow involved. He thought that perhaps it was time for him to make some enquiries of his own. In the meantime he suggested that Tricia should make careful preparations for the announced inspection. 'Not that you will need to do anything special,' he said. 'I know the home runs on well oiled wheels and the inspection cannot be a problem.' Tricia thanked him for his support and showed him out. Afterwards she said good night to the residents and drove home to share her worries with her husband.

Chapter Twenty-Seven

As Christmas drew nearer the weather got a lot colder and there were some heavy frosts in the mornings. The Christmas shopping trip proved to be a great success; Mrs Hargreaves was still in hospital and the four older residents said they didn't want to go, so the remaining thirteen set off after coffee with Tim and Paula. 'Oh dear,' said Harriet as she climbed into the minibus, 'I hope that because there are thirteen of us it won't prove to be unlucky.'

'I don't know what you mean,' said Jerry. 'If we include Tim and Paula there are actually fifteen of us. Anyway I've always believed that you make your own luck.'

'Except in Harry's case,' said Glyn. 'He mixes luck with some kind of magic to produce winners of horse races.'

'Nonsense,' said the Major, 'it isn't magic, it's called studying form and using one's intelligence.'

The minibus reached the market town, which was their destination at about eleven-thirty. Paula suggested that they should wander round the town in small groups to do some shopping. She asked them all to meet in the Red Lion, which was in the main street, at one o'clock. She added that she had arranged with the landlord to provide lunch and asked them not to be late, looking specifically at the liar dice group.

The Major took his three companions into a betting office and introduced them to some of the mysteries of studying form with the newspaper called the *Racing Post*. The whole group duly assembled at the Red Lion and had a very pleasant lunch of roast chicken with all the trimmings followed by traditional Christmas pudding and mince pies. Paula had ordered three bottles of wine with the meal and the landlord then brought out a further three bottles which he insisted were on the house.

As some of the ladies drank very little, the men saw it as their solemn duty not to waste any of the wine. They sat in the pub playing the inevitable liar dice while the ladies went off to do some more shopping. By three o'clock their moods varied from mellow to merry and as Tim and Paula ushered them out to the minibus Tim whispered that he thought one or two malt whiskies had followed the wine.

On the journey home some of the ladies started to sing carols and Jerry and the Major joined in lustily. Glyn and Vic both seemed to be dozing and one of the other male residents, Peter Banks, was snoring quite loudly.

'Goodness me,' said Paula, 'the alcohol fumes in here are enough to get me drunk, never mind them.'

The party mood continued into the evening and by bedtime everybody was well and truly in the Christmas mood.

Chapter Twenty-Eight

As the 21st of December and the announced inspection drew near, the Major noticed that the toilet rolls kept disappearing from the men's lavatories. He discussed this with his fellow members of the liar dice team and they concluded that someone was deliberately removing the toilet rolls in order to cause trouble. 'I've a pretty good idea who's responsible,' said the Major. 'We won't worry Tricia about it.' He then made a suggestion which the others thought both ingenious and acceptable and readily agreed to participate involving the other men in the home.

Paula and Tricia were making sure that their records were scrupulously up to date and Lucy and the care staff were ensuring that everywhere was up to the usual high standard of cleanliness and order. The dreaded day dawned and James Slighe presented himself promptly at eight-thirty just as most residents were finishing breakfast. He was accompanied by Mrs Phillips and Miss Burley and a thin, pale man whom he introduced as his deputy, Mr Heap. Tricia had met Mr Heap at some in-service seminars and had always regarded him as a reasonable man although she had heard that he was now completely dominated and manipulated by James Slighe.

As all five of them sat in the office James Slighe fired his opening salvo: 'As we came up the drive,' he said, 'I noticed that there was a pond in the front garden and more importantly that it wasn't fenced off.'

Tricia was surprised but said that the pond was only about nine inches deep and she didn't see that it needed fencing.

'Ah,' said Slighe, 'supposing one of the residents tripped and fell in face down, they could quite easily drown.'

Tricia replied that the pond had been there for fifteen years since the home opened and there had never been any kind of mishap.

'Nevertheless,' said Slighe, 'it should be fenced off and I shall say so in my report.'

He then said that Mrs Phillips and Miss Burley would inspect the records whilst he and Mr Heap inspected the house. 'Perhaps you could get one of your male staff to accompany us,' he said.

Tricia replied that she would get Tim, but Slighe said, 'No I don't think that long-haired fellow is acceptable. What about your new man, Mr Pratt.'

Again Tricia was rather surprised but she duly went and collected Ken Pratt and asked him to accompany the two inspectors. During the inspection they made a point of inspecting all the fire closing equipment on the doors. On two of them the screws appeared to be very loose and in consequence the doors would not shut properly.

'Make a note of that,' said Slighe to his deputy. 'Now lets have a look at the bathrooms.' Whilst they were looking round the bathrooms and lavatories Slighe spotted that there were no toilet rolls in the men's lavatories and Ken Pratt muttered something to him.

In the meantime the residents were attempting to go around and continue their lives as normal and when Pratt and the inspectors pushed open Glyn's door he was quite angry and said, 'Bugger off, this is private.' Slighe explained that they were looking round all the rooms and Glyn replied, 'Not this one,' and slammed the door in their face.

Pratt said to the inspectors, 'There are quite a few stroppy men here and the problem is that Mrs Beasley has no control over them.'

The inspection eventually finished and James Slighe asked if they could all meet in the sitting room with the residents. Tricia replied that she would ask the residents, although she knew that two or three of them had gone out and that one or two of the older residents would not wish to be involved.

'No,' said Slighe, 'I've already gathered that your residents are a stroppy bunch, perhaps it's the way the staff treat them.'

Tricia was totally dumbfounded and turning to Paula, who was accompanying her, said, 'I think we've got a lovely group of residents.' Paula agreed.

Slighe said, 'Well, you would say that anyway.'

About ten of the residents gathered in the sitting room with the inspectors and the staff and Tricia had made sure that coffee and biscuits were provided for everyone, even though it was almost lunchtime. James Slighe introduced his companions and explained to the residents that they only inspected homes to make sure that the residents were properly cared for.

Jerry said, 'I think we've had this conversation before and we all agree that this is a super home and we are extremely happy.'

Slighe said, 'I'm glad to hear that, nevertheless there are a few problems which we need to look at. For example, I'm told that it is custom and practice not to provide toilet rolls in the men's lavatories.'

Tricia looked aghast but before she could say anything Glyn said, 'Custom and practice, my ass, somebody keeps pinching the damn things.'

And the Major said, 'However, it isn't a problem because all the men have toilet rolls in their own bedrooms which they can take with them if the others have vanished.'

Vic then interposed and said, 'May we ask who said that

it is custom and practice not to have loo rolls?' and Slighe replied that he was not at liberty to divulge such information. The Major happened to catch Ken Pratt's eye and received a look of pure venom.

There was further discussion, most of which was negative and eventually Slighe looked at his watch and said, 'Well, it is almost one o'clock. I expect you will be wanting your lunch? May my colleagues and I wish you all a very merry Christmas?'

And as they turned to go out Glyn said, 'Sarcastic bugger.' Tricia attempted to get some feedback as the inspectors were leaving but she was told that she would receive their report in due course.

Chapter Twenty-Nine

By the 23rd of December most of the residents were getting quite excited, but Tricia and her staff were finding it difficult to concentrate on the festivities. Paula came in looking very worried saying that she had had a telephone call at home yesterday evening. This was Miss Burley, one of the inspectors who had visited, and she asked Paula if she was happy at Hollytree House and if there were any problems or anxieties she would like to share. Paula had apparently given her very short shrift but was worried as to why she had been singled out for such a telephone call. 'Perhaps you haven't been singled out,' said Tricia. 'It may be that there will be other similar calls.'

After lunch that day the Major went into the kitchen and asked Mrs Halliday if he could have a flask of coffee as he wanted to go down and talk to Andy about the Millennium party. When he got down to the hut the door was closed because he hadn't realised that Andy had finished work at lunchtime that day. He opened the door to check if Andy was inside and suddenly felt a tremendous thump in his back; this propelled him across the shed where he hit his head on a shelf and fell to the floor. The door was then slammed shut and the bolts rammed firmly in place.

Although he was semi-conscious he thought he heard a voice say, 'That will teach you to be such a clever bugger, you and your toilet rolls.'

*

At teatime Jerry asked where the Major was and Vic said, 'Oh he's probably found a couple of winners and he's waiting to collect his winnings in the betting shop.' However at dinnertime he still hadn't reappeared and Jerry asked Paula where the Major had got to.

'I've no idea,' replied Paula, 'he didn't tell me he was going out.' When she asked everyone at dinner if they had any idea where the Major had gone nobody had any ideas.

'I expect he'll be back soon,' said Vic, 'he's probably gone to the pub to celebrate his winnings, lucky devil.'

'We don't know if he had any winnings,' said Jerry. 'We don't know whether he even went to the betting office.'

By suppertime they were all getting a bit alarmed. Paula called Tricia, who came in and said she would ring the other staff to see if the Major had said anything to them. She didn't normally include the cooks in this sort of problem but as everyone was now so worried she rang Mrs Halliday, who was on the afternoon shift, and asked her if she had any ideas. 'Well, all I know,' said Mrs Halliday, 'is that he asked me for a flask of coffee about half-past two and usually when he does that he goes down to see Andy.' Tricia relayed this information to Paula, who said, 'Andy wasn't on this afternoon.'

Tricia called Tim and they got a couple of torches and went down the long path leading to the gardener's hut. They shone the torches as they walked but saw nothing untoward and when they got to the hut Tim said, 'Well he can't be in there; look, it's bolted from the outside.'

They started to turn away but as they did so Tricia thought that she heard a groan. 'What was that,' she said. 'I think we may as well take a look in the hut now we're down here.' They unbolted the door and as they shone their torches inside they saw the Major lying on the floor with blood all over his face.

'Oh my God, run to the house, Tim, and call an ambulance,' cried Tricia. She went into the hut and knelt beside the Major. She was almost in tears but she whispered to him, 'Can you hear me, Harry?' The Major groaned and mumbled something and she carefully wiped some of the blood from his face. It was obvious that he had a large cut across his forehead where he had collided with the shelf. The ambulance arrived very promptly and the paramedics very carefully carried the Major to the ambulance. 'I'm coming with him,' said Tricia, and asked Tim if he would phone her husband and explain what had happened.

Tim went back into the house and after he had made the telephone call he tried to explain to the others what had happened.

'Perhaps he tripped and fell accidentally,' said Jerry.

'Yes,' said Tim, 'but then he got up and bolted the door from the outside.'

CHAPTER THIRTY

Christmas Eve was a cold, brisk day with a watery sun trying to liven up the proceedings. At breakfast however there was no mention of Christmas, the sole topic of conversation was the Major and his very unfortunate accident. Not that anyone believed that it had been an accident.

'It's obvious,' said Jerry, 'that he couldn't possibly have locked himself in; I went down there before breakfast and there are two bolts on the outside of the door.'

'Right,' said Glyn, 'then we have to conclude that he was obviously attacked by someone.'

Paula overheard this conversation and said, 'Nobody must go down there again; Tricia has reported the matter to the police and they will obviously want to investigate what they call the scene of crime.'

Vic asked Paula where Tricia was and had she got any news about Harry. Paula replied that Tricia had gone home to get some rest as she had been at the hospital until about two-thirty a.m. She said that Harry had needed some stitches in his head but when she left he was asleep. She also said that he insisted on coming home and providing the hospital staff agreed, she and Tim would be going to pick him up in the afternoon.

Just then the doorbell rang and when Paula opened the door there was a young police constable and a pleasant young woman who introduced herself as Detective Sergeant Wilkins. Paula asked Tim to take them down the garden and show them the shed where the incident had occurred.

Later that morning the Scene of Crimes Officer arrived looking for evidence. The residents were excited and spent a lot of time looking out of the windows and talking nineteen to the dozen, as Lucy rather quaintly put it.

In the afternoon the Major was collected from the hospital and arrived at Hollytree House looking rather pale with his head swathed in a large bandage. The residents made a fuss of him until he said that he had a headache and if they didn't mind he would like to go to his room for a while and lie down.

Later, he came downstairs for a cup of tea and whilst he was chatting to the other residents Paula came in bringing his son, George. George was very concerned and explained to his father that he couldn't get there sooner because he had been in Manchester overnight. He had only heard from Isabel when he had got home at lunchtime. He then went on to say, 'Isabel and I would like you to come home for Christmas.' At this, the Major's face lost even more colour, the thought of being at Isabel's mercy over the holiday period was too much to contemplate.

'That's very kind of you, George,' he said, 'but I wouldn't like to put you to any trouble and I will be quite happy here with my new friends.' Although George pressed him again, the Major was sure that he was relieved and he eventually took his leave saying that he would call in again on Boxing Day.

Chapter Thirty-One

As the evening approached there was still an air of great excitement and the staff spent a lot of time calming down the residents, whilst the liar dice team not only decided who was the culprit but what in their opinion ought to be done to him. About seven o'clock a group of mainly young people came from the local church to sing carols and Tricia, who was now back on duty, thought that perhaps the Christmas spirit was being revived. Everybody had mulled wine and mince pies and the young visitors made their farewells.

Most of the ladies were very nervous and said that they were definitely going to lock their doors. Tricia said that under the circumstances both she and Tim would be sleeping in and Mrs Jenkins, the waking staff, would be very alert. She assured all the residents that there was no need to worry and Vic said, 'Well, at least we can be grateful that Pratt is not on duty, I wouldn't trust him as far as I could throw him. It was almost certainly him that attacked Harry.' Tricia said that it was wrong to jump to conclusions and the police thought that it might have been somebody intending to steal tools from the shed.

She would have been more disturbed had she known that a police inspector with the improbable name of Snurge had telephoned James Slighe that afternoon. They had discussed the incident at Hollytree House and Slighe immediately suspected who might be behind the assault. However, he told Snurge that some of the male residents were aggressive old troublemakers and that the woman who was supposed to be in charge had no control over them. He said that it could have been one of the residents who attacked the injured party.

As it happened Inspector Snurge was another member of the same club as Slighe and the other plotters. He assured Slighe that he would keep him informed and added that he had a new Detective Sergeant on the job who was quite a nice young woman, but perhaps a bit too keen for her own good.

However, Tricia was blissfully unaware of this development and she and the other staff eventually got the residents into their rooms just before midnight. She and Tim then went down to the kitchen and over a cup of cocoa discussed some of the recent events. Tim was quite sure that a lot of the problems revolved around Ken Pratt. Tricia, on the other hand, felt that the real problem had begun even before Ken Pratt had arrived and she wondered just why they were having so much trouble. They realised that it was now one a.m. and decided to leave any further discussion for another day. Mrs Jenkins wished them both goodnight and said they had obviously had a very long day and it was time for them to leave the rest of the night in her capable hands.

Chapter Thirty-Two

Christmas morning proved to be cold and wet and although Harriet and her three friends said that they wanted to go to church, everybody else decided to stay at home. Jerry said that as far as he was concerned the best Christmas spirit came out of a bottle and he would rather sit and be comfortable at home rather than sit in a cold, draughty church. After breakfast Christmas presents were handed round. Vic and Poppy had volunteered two or three weeks earlier to collect money from all the residents so that they could give all the staff a small present.

Most of the staff wanted to be at home for Christmas Day with their own families but Tim, who was single, said he wasn't bothered as he would much rather celebrate New Year. Tricia had arranged for her husband, Robbie, to come in and help out. Tim took the four ladies to church but he did not go in, telling them that he would be back later to collect them after the service. He returned to Hollytree House where he joined the other residents for coffee and more mince pies.

Lunch was a very pleasant affair and although Mrs Halliday and Mrs Burton weren't in they had left everything ready for a full Christmas dinner with all the trimmings. While Tricia and Tim worked in the kitchen, Robbie acted as butler and had a joke and a smile for everyone. Jerry volunteered to be the wine waiter and poured very generous drinks as Mr Khan's financial contribution meant that they had ordered two cases of very decent wine. Tricia ensured that one case was safely put away for the Millennium party and Jerry said, a bit reluctantly, that he thought twelve bottles might just be enough for Christmas Day.

The Major sat in the corner of the sitting room; he still looked very pale and murmured to Tricia that he had an appalling headache. Tricia found him some painkillers and spent the rest of the day keeping a very careful eye on him and asked Tim to do the same. Some of the ladies had planned to visit Mrs Hargreaves in hospital during the afternoon but when Tricia telephoned the hospital she was told that Mrs Hargreaves was unconscious and very poorly.

'We are not having much luck at the moment,' said Tricia to her husband.

He reassured her and said, 'Hollytree House is a very good home and with you in charge everything will soon be back on a normal basis.'

Chapter Thirty-Three

Boxing Day was on a Sunday and so the house was very quiet and most of the residents seemed rather subdued. Tricia did not expect to hear anything from the police until after the Christmas holiday but in the afternoon Sergeant Wilkins called round. She said that she was interested to know how the residents were coping with the assault and whether Tricia had gleaned any information from their discussions. Tricia explained that most of the staff would not be back on duty until Tuesday. She asked Sergeant Wilkins whether the Scene of Crime Officer had found anything but Sergeant Wilkins replied that she was afraid there was very little evidence to be found.

She asked Tricia if the Major had any enemies among the other residents and whether one of them could be responsible. Tricia was extremely surprised and said that on the contrary the Major was extremely popular. She asked Sergeant Wilkins why she had asked the question. The Sergeant replied, 'Well, I shouldn't be saying this and I hope it will remain confidential between us, but my boss seems to think that it was an inside job and one of the other residents was probably responsible.' Tricia said that she thought this was highly unlikely, certainly none of the ladies could have pushed the Major with such force and as she had already said he was popular with the men. Sergeant Wilkins took her leave, assuring Tricia that she would do everything she could to catch the culprit.

As she was going out of the door she said, 'What about the staff?'

Tricia explained that there were only three men: Andy, the part time gardener, who was a great friend of the Major's, Tim, her third in charge, in whom she had every confidence, and a relatively new man, Ken Pratt, who was serving a probationary period. She noticed that the Detective Sergeant seemed to recognise the name Ken Pratt and was not surprised when the Sergeant said that she would come back on Tuesday and interview the male staff and the residents.

Two of the residents, Peter Banks and Millicent Dean, had visitors during the afternoon but most of the residents had simply received Christmas cards or letters from their relatives.

The members of the liar dice team discussed the lack of interest from the families of the residents. Jerry summed it up by saying that no one really wants you when you're old.

'Aye,' said Glyn, 'But when you snuff it you can bet the buggers come out of the woodwork to see if you've left any money.'

As Sunday drew to a close, an air of gloom and melancholy seemed to settle over Hollytree House.

Chapter Thirty-Four

Monday was still a bank holiday as Boxing Day had fallen on the Sunday. The male residents were a bit disturbed because although there was racing from Kempton Park on the television, the Major showed very little interest. Jerry said to Paula that he thought the Major was not at all well and Paula had a note which Tricia had left asking her to keep a particularly close eye on him. The news from the hospital regarding Mrs Hargreaves was still not good and the Christmas holidays seemed to have collapsed in a rather disappointing way.

On Tuesday Sergeant Wilkins arrived bringing with her two constables, one male and one female. They asked Tricia if they could have three rooms where they could interview the staff and residents. Tricia suggested that they use the music room, the dining room and her office, and Sergeant Wilkins said that she thought it would be a good idea if Tricia was willing to sit in on the interviews that the young woman police constable was conducting with the female residents. The male constable would interview the male residents in the dining room and she herself would interview the staff in the music room.

The interviews in the office went very quietly and although some of the ladies expressed their nervousness they were unable to provide any useful information. The interviews in the dining room, however, were much more lively. The young constable received a number of theories and suggestions and one specific name kept cropping up. When the Major was interviewed he said that he remembered as the door slammed a male voice made a comment about toilet rolls. The constable noted this down but couldn't imagine how it could be relevant.

Sergeant Wilkins interviewed the staff in the music room and felt that she got very little information, although all the staff were pleasant and helpful. Ken Pratt was at his most charming but Sergeant Wilkins nevertheless felt rather uneasy in his presence; his eyes seemed to roam constantly over her body and she found herself pulling her skirt down and keeping her knees together. Tim and Andy both expressed genuine concern and the young sergeant was quite sure that neither of them could be the culprit. None of the female staff would have had any reason to attack the Major and there was nothing missing from the shed. The sergeant knew that any theories she may have would have to be endorsed by her very authoritarian boss, Inspector Snurge. After the interviews the three police staff met with Tricia in her office and thanked her for her co-operation. She asked them if they had come to any conclusions but Sergeant Wilkins said that they would have to compare notes and obviously couldn't make any statements at this time.

Chapter Thirty-Five

On Wednesday morning at breakfast there was still a very subdued atmosphere. Tricia was unhappy about this and said to Paula and Tim that they really had to do something to lift the residents' spirits. She thought that it would be a good idea to call a meeting and start planning the Millennium party for Friday evening. 'I know that you won't be here,' she said to Tim, 'but I would like you to help with the planning.' Tim replied that he had been intending to go away for the New Year but under the circumstances he felt that he ought to stay. 'That would be great,' said Tricia and Paula in unison and Tricia realised that Tim obviously cared as much about the residents as she did.

They decided to have a meeting with the residents after coffee and when Tricia explained to everybody the reason for the meeting, everyone seemed to brighten up and ideas started to flow. Tricia asked the residents if it would be acceptable for the staff that were attending to bring their partners and there was almost unanimous agreement for this.

However, Jerry then spoke up and said, 'I don't want to be difficult but we have discussed the matter and agreed that we don't want Pratt at the party.' Vic concurred and said that in view of what had happened to the Major it would be impossible for them to accept Ken Pratt at their celebrations.

After a whispered discussion with Paula, Tricia said that although she did not think that there was any evidence to hold

Ken Pratt responsible for the assault on the Major, she did understand how the residents felt. She said that when Mr Pratt came in for the afternoon shift she would suggest to him he had a week's leave. The residents applauded and it was quite obvious that there was no doubt whom the residents blamed for the assault on the Major.

Tim then said that he had three mates who were a music trio and he was quite sure that he could persuade them to play at the party, even if it was New Year's Eve. 'Mind you,' he said, 'we will have to make sure that we keep the beer flowing as they get very thirsty when they play.'

Harriet suggested that they should make it an impromptu fancy dress party and after some discussion everyone went off in a much happier frame of mind, planning what they would wear.

In the afternoon Paula took Harriet, Joyce and Willy to see Mrs Hargreaves. She had again regained consciousness but was very weak and could say very little. They had agreed in advance not to mention the Millennium party because it was obvious that she would not be able to attend. As they left the hospital Harriet said, 'Poor soul, she hasn't got long for this world,' and there were a few tears and sniffles on the drive back to the home.

To Tricia's relief, Ken Pratt eagerly accepted the offer of a week's leave. 'We've got a party planned at the TA Centre and it should be a real good booze up,' he said. 'Besides, I've had just about enough of these old buggers glaring at me and muttering to each other. I do hope that you don't believe that I was responsible for the assault on that silly old sod.'

Tricia replied that she had no intention of blaming anyone at this stage as there was no proof. 'However,' she added, 'I do not think you should talk about the residents in such a disrespectful way.'

'I don't see why,' he retorted. 'They don't show me any respect.'

'Respect has to be earned,' said Tricia.

He mumbled what might have been an apology and left the office. When Tricia got home that night she recounted the day's events to Robbie and not for the first time thought how lucky she was to have such an understanding husband.

Chapter Thirty-six

Hollytree House was a hive of activity all day on Thursday. Some of the men started to put up extra decorations as the preparations for the Christmas festivities had been rather subdued. Harriet and her friends were busy making impromptu costumes and Mrs Halliday and Mrs Burton, the two cooks, volunteered to work all day to provide special food for the party. Tim and Andy went into town to purchase a supply of beer and other drinks to complement the saved case of wine. It was decided that as the sitting room was the biggest area it would be the best place for dancing. This meant that most of the furniture had to be moved into the music room to make sufficient space. The male residents volunteered to do this but Tricia kept an anxious eye on them and insisted that they left the heaviest furniture for Tim and Andy to move.

The Major helped but found that he had to sit down frequently because of a severe headache. After lunch the doorbell rang and when Tricia answered it she found Sergeant Wilkins standing on the step. 'My goodness,' said the Sergeant when she stood in the hall and observed all the activity. Tricia explained that they were preparing for the Millennium party. 'It's really great to see all these elderly people so obviously enjoying themselves,' said the Sergeant. 'I hope that I find a home like this when I've retired.'

Tricia laughed and said, 'That's a long way off,' and then

she asked the detective if there was a specific reason for her visit.

She replied by saying, 'Perhaps we could go into your office,' and when they went in she shut the door firmly behind them.

She explained that she was in something of a dilemma and asked Tricia if she could be assured of complete confidentiality. Tricia agreed and the sergeant then went on to explain that she was being heavily leaned on by her boss, Inspector Snurge. 'He insists,' she said, 'that we conclude that whoever attacked Major Webb must have been an intruder who was intending to steal some of the tools from the shed.' Tricia remarked it sounded as if Sergeant Wilkins would not be happy with that conclusion. The Sergeant replied that if it were her decision she would like to question Mr Pratt a little more fully down at the station. 'However,' she added, 'that must be strictly between us.'

Tricia told her that she had given Pratt a week's leave because of the residents request that he should not attend the party. 'I can sympathise with them,' said the Sergeant. 'I am sure that he was involved in the assault on the Major but it looks as if he will get away with it. It seems as if my hands are tied because I have only just been promoted and can be easily overruled and, as you know, they don't have women in the funny handshake club.' Tricia was very sympathetic and explained that Ken Pratt was supposed to be transferring to the Haven. She added that she would try to make the move sooner rather than later. Sergeant Wilkins took her leave and after she had left, Tricia went to see how the preparations were going.

*

Several of the residents were very secretive about their fancy dress plans and there was an air of expectation and excitement throughout the home. By suppertime everybody seemed very tired and Tricia suggested that they should have an early night as tomorrow would be very hectic. There was no dissent and everybody moved gradually off to their own rooms.

Chapter Thirty-Seven

New Year's Eve was a bright, crisp day with a tinge of hoar frost, making the garden look particularly pleasant. The residents were obviously very excited and Tricia thought, as she had many times in the past, how the wheel of life seemed to go full circle. She thought that her residents were probably just as animated and excited now as they had been when they were small children preparing for a party. She and Tim were a skeleton staff crew because most of the others were coming in for the party in the evening. She couldn't help hoping that there would be no callers from the inspectorate, as they would obviously perceive the situation as a problem.

There were, however, no unwelcome visitors and the day sped by with a scratch lunch and a very light tea as everybody was saving their appetite for the evening. Mrs Burton, who was a widow, came in at about four o'clock and started moving food into the dining room. 'Mrs Halliday will be along a little later with her husband,' she said, 'but I thought I would make a start'.

By six o'clock there was loud music and lots of cheerful laughter and even the Major seemed to have temporarily forgotten his headaches.

Just before seven, Tim's friends, who were the band members, arrived and started setting up their instruments in the corner of the room. Poppy and Vic were very excited because they planned to announce their engagement that evening and only Poppy's three friends knew that this was likely to happen. It had been decided that there would be music and dancing between seven-thirty and nine-thirty p.m. and then everyone would retire to the dining room for the very splendid buffet which was being provided. About eight-thirty the liar dice group disappeared and came back a few minutes later dressed as a barber shop quartet. With a very quiet backing from the band they sang a number of songs from the 1930's and 40's and everybody applauded enthusiastically.

There were all sorts of costumes on view; from Harriet dressed as Madame Pompadour through to Joyce who appeared in her old Women's Land Army uniform. Willy, however, stole the show dressed as Calamity Jane, complete with whip, and she laughed with everyone else when Jerry said, 'Oh, its Miss Whiplash.' There was no doubt that everybody was having a very good time and at nine-thirty they went into the dining room.

In addition to the residents, seven of the staff had brought their partners and with the band there were just about forty people. However, there was enough food to feed twice that number and Paula said jokingly, 'We'll all be eating left-overs for a week.' After everybody had eaten their fill and several of the gentlemen had drunk more than was probably good for them, they returned to the sitting room and the band struck up again. Jerry remarked that the one noticeable absentee was Bridie, and he for one was sorry about that because he had looked forward to dancing with her. Glyn suggested that her husband had probably forbidden her to come as he was apparently a very jealous man.

At about fifteen minutes before midnight Vic called for silence and said that he had an important announcement to make. He then went on to take Poppy's hand and announce that they had become engaged to be married. Everybody applauded wildly and Tricia thought, 'Oh Lord, another headache!'

All too soon it was time for the midnight hour to strike and everybody went out onto the lawn to listen to the church bells. The staff had great difficulty in persuading some of the residents to put on their topcoats, as it was very cold. Tim put on the floodlights and when the church bells started to ring out for the New Year everybody joined hands and sang Auld Lang Syne.

Tricia fervently hoped that the new Millennium would bring good luck to Hollytree House. Her husband, Robbie, must have guessed what she was thinking because he put his arm around her and said, 'Cheer up, darling, it's going to be a good year. Now you have got a wedding to look forward to'. Tricia replied that she was very pleased for Vic and Poppy but she knew that some people would think it very strange for two elderly people to be getting married. 'I can't see why,' said Robbie. 'They are obviously in love and they both look very happy.' Eventually everybody moved back into the house, the staff and their partners made their farewells and the residents gradually meandered off to bed. The Major was one of the last to go and when he eventually settled down he spent a few minutes ruminating over the past few months. He too hoped that the New Year would be better. 'And I'm sure it will be,' he said to himself, then drifted off into a deep and dreamless sleep.

Chapter Thirty-Eight

The first two weeks of the new year were quiet and uneventful. For a few days after the party most of the residents relived the fun of it all. Some of the reminiscences were developed and became more highly coloured with the retelling. Jerry in particular enjoyed exaggerating stories including a highly dubious one, which involved him catching Glyn and Joyce in a passionate embrace in the kitchen. They both repudiated the story, Joyce very vehemently, but Glyn eventually admitted to the other men that perhaps he had a little too much to drink and got a bit carried away.

The staff settled down and although Ken Pratt returned to work he was very subdued and careful not to offend anyone. He and Tricia had a long discussion and it was agreed that he would move to the Haven at the end of the month. The Major started studying the form of race horses again and he told the other members of the liar dice club that he had started to work on his Cheltenham selections for the middle of March. He told them that he was determined to get the 'Cheltenham four' this year.

On the 17th of January Tricia had to convey some very bad news to the staff and residents. This concerned Mrs Hargreaves, who had lapsed into a coma early in the new year and the hospital had telephoned to say that she had unfortunately died. Naturally everyone was very upset and without exception they said that they all wanted to go to the funeral. Two of Mrs Hargreaves' daughters made a very rare visit and looked over the contents of her room. As they were leaving Glyn said, 'Bloody vultures, they hardly ever came when she was alive.' Jerry added that as he had said before, no one wants you when you're old. The Major said that growing old was like being on a battlefield; all your friends are dead or dying. He went on to say that he sometimes thought that those soldiers he knew who had been killed were the lucky ones. 'They have never had to suffer the misery of old age,' he said.

'Talking of relatives,' said Vic, 'your son hasn't been to see you since Christmas Eve.'

'Ah well,' said the Major, 'he and Isabel are planning to move to New Zealand so they are very busy.'

Vic said, 'That's largely the trouble; very few people, including relatives, really care about the plight of the elderly. The Government goes on interminably about education but those of us who served in the war and those of us who have worked hard all our lives are ignored and neglected.'

'That's true,' said Glyn. 'How many elderly people die every year because they don't get enough to eat or are unable to keep warm.'

'Aye,' said Jerry, 'fat lot of help we get from the Government. The trouble with modern politicians is that they don't care about the people. They are too busy building up their power bases or feathering their nests.'

'I agree with you all,' said the Major, 'but our main concern at the moment is the future of Hollytree House and the welfare of the residents. If we don't look after ourselves nobody else will.'

Chapter Thirty-Nine

Mrs Hargreaves' funeral took place on Friday the 21st of January. It was a bright, pleasant morning and she was buried in a quiet country churchyard, which was in the village where she had lived as a child. She had specifically asked for her favourite hymn, *Morning has Broken*, to be sung at her funeral and the small congregation sang it with gusto. All the residents had been transported to the village and Tricia had arranged for them to have a simple lunch afterwards in the local pub, which was called the Coach and Horses.

Some of the men said they would walk from the churchyard to the pub and as they walked down the main street they passed the primary school, which Paula said Mrs Hargreaves had attended. It was lunchtime and as they passed the schoolyard a number of children rushed out to play. Almost without thinking the Major said to Jerry, 'It's very strange to think that a few years ago Mrs Hargreaves was playing in that schoolyard and now she's buried in the churchyard.'

'It was quite a few years ago, old boy,' replied Jerry. 'After all, she was well into her eighties.'

'Nevertheless,' said the Major, 'I find it very disconcerting to look at the very young and the very old in the same context; life is so very brief. It is almost as if those children we just saw are the ghosts of Mrs Hargreaves and her friends.'

'Oh come on,' said Jerry, 'cheer up. I'll buy you a large whisky,' but as he ushered the Major through the pub doors he too felt a strange sense of melancholy because of the way the Major spoke.

Three of Mrs Hargreaves' relatives joined them for lunch and made an effort to talk to the residents. Tricia and Paula couldn't help feeling that perhaps they should have made more effort when Mrs Hargreaves was alive.

After lunch they all made their way back to Hollytree House. The group in the minibus were very subdued and Tricia thought that they must be thinking, 'who will be next to go?' She herself found that days such as this were the hardest part of her job. She befriended the residents and grew to love them, but all the time was conscious that sooner or later they would have to die. There were times when she wondered how long she could continue with her job. She always felt a real sense of loss when one of the residents died. On the other hand, she consoled herself that she was helping them to enjoy their last few years of life.

*

The evening was equally quiet and, as he had another of his now frequently recurring headaches, the Major made his excuses and went to bed immediately after supper. Jerry remarked to Glyn and Vic that he thought perhaps the Major had not got over his accident. 'I'm not surprised,' said Glyn, 'and for Pete's sake stop calling it an accident; it was a nasty vicious assault by a nasty vicious lout. If there is any justice he will get his comeuppance.'

jumped to the wrong conclusions. Bridie hastily rang off but what made it worse was that when her husband dialled 1471 he got the disembodied operator's voice telling him that the caller had withheld their number. He said that she was obviously 'carrying on' and attacked her.

'But this is outrageous,' said the Major. 'How dare they call you at home? For one thing they could not identify themselves over the telephone and it could have been anyone.' Bridie dried her eyes and said that she must get on.

The Major rushed into Tricia's office and told her about his conversation with Bridie. Tricia said that she had already spoken to Bridie and she suspected that they had called several members of staff, although only Paula had confirmed it. 'But that kind of behaviour is disgusting,' said the Major. 'It is not only sly and underhand but surely it is against any decent principles of social work.'

'I'm afraid I agree with you,' said Tricia, 'but I don't understand what is going on and why they seem to be conducting a campaign against Hollytree House.'

'Well perhaps we should find out,' said the Major. 'I know we are only a bunch of old fogies but it is our home and we may be able to help.'

'I'm supposed to be looking after you,' said Tricia, 'but I do feel rather helpless at the moment and if there is any way you or any of the other residents can help then I shall be grateful.' The minute the words were out of her mouth, she felt guilty and incompetent. 'Look Major,' she went on, 'you must not feel that you have to worry, it is my problem and I will resolve it somehow.'

'Of course,' he replied, 'but it is our home and our future and we should help if we can.'

CHAPTER FOR[TY]

The last week of the month saw hostilities being resume[d as] the Major charged into Tricia's office with all guns bla[zing]. Although he was not one of Bridie's bath customers – h[e was] still too reserved for that – they had become good fri[ends]. She often sat with him and they would chat about all so[rts of] things. One of their favourite topics was Ireland; the [Major] and his wife had been to the west coast on several occa[sions] for holidays and he confided to Bridie that they had th[oughts] of retiring there.

On this occasion, however, they sat in the music roo[m and] did not talk about Ireland. Bridie had been off for a cou[ple of] days and when she came in on this particular morning sh[e had] a split lip and bruises around her eyes. When the Major a[sked] her what had happened she said at first that she had w[alked] into a door, but he would not accept this. When he presse[d her] her eyes filled with tears and she said that her husband [had] punched her in the face. 'The vicious swine,' said the M[ajor]. He should be horsewhipped.' But Bridie said that it w[as not] entirely his fault.

Apparently she had been at home three evenings ea[rlier] and when she answered the telephone it was a man who [said] he was from Social Services and he wondered if she had [any] difficulties at work or if there was anything she would li[ke to] share with him about the problems of Hollytree House. [Her] husband overheard part of the conversation and immedi[ately]

Chapter Forty-One

Later that day the Major asked the liar dice club and the bridge ladies to meet with him in the music room. He told them about Bridie and explained the situation as far as he knew from Tricia, and asked the other seven if they would help him to save Hollytree House. He went on to say that it may sound dramatic but it looked as if someone was trying to close their home down.

Everybody started talking at once until Jerry said, 'Slow down, people, let's discuss this calmly.'

Harriet said that she had a good friend who was a retired solicitor and she would ask him what the legal situation was and whether the home could be closed down.

Whilst this discussion was going on Tricia was in her office opening a brown envelope which had been delivered by hand. In it there were a number of official looking notices, which indicated that certain rules and regulations had been broken. She was amazed to see that the first one referred to the fireguard in the music room despite the fact that she and Paula had explained that the fire was never used. The notice said that she had ignored the need for a fireguard.

The second one was similar in that there were three radiators in the hall and on the landing which were not covered with guards. Again she had explained that when the new oil-fired central heating had been fitted these three radiators, which had been powered by Calor gas, had become redundant and were simply waiting to be dismantled.

The third notice referred to the fence around the pond. After Tricia had been told that the pond had to be fenced off Andy had erected a neat green trellis about eighteen inches high around the pond. The notice said that this was not a proper fence as the residents could still fall over it.

The fourth notice concerned the residents' access to the garden shed and said that it must be made quite clear to the residents that that area was out of bounds.

Tricia didn't know whether to laugh or cry at the stupidity of the notices but she became very upset when she read the accompanying letter. This stated that in view of the fact that two residents had died recently and a third one had been subjected to a vicious assault there were grave doubts about whether the residents of Hollytree House were being properly cared for. When she came to the end of the letter Tricia burst into tears and sat behind her desk sobbing quietly.

Chapter Forty-Two

As Tricia sat there the door of her office suddenly opened and she quickly dabbed her eyes with a tissue and tried to look composed. However, it was Paula who was just coming on duty and she immediately realised that Tricia was very upset. She asked Tricia what the problem was and without speaking Tricia handed over the notices and the letter. Paula sat and very quietly read them and when Tricia looked at her, her face had gone very red and she looked as if she was about to explode. 'This is wicked,' she said. 'How can they possibly suggest that the deaths of Mrs Hargreaves and Old Tom were due to anything but natural causes, and we'd all like to know exactly what happened to the Major. In any case I'm sure our GP, Dr Weller will confirm that we have very few house calls. The last time he came to see Mrs Hargreaves he remarked on that very fact. He also said that he thought our residents were very well cared for.'

They sat in silence for a few minutes and then Paula said 'By the way, did you notice in the book that I'd written about a telephone conversation I had yesterday?'

Tricia had to confess that for once she hadn't read yesterday's log and Paula said, 'Well I suppose you've got a lot on your mind at the moment. Anyway,' she said, 'the call was from a Social Services inspector in the Black Country. This chap said that he had heard from his opposite number in our authority that there were some serious problems and he was sending a social worker down to see if the resident from their authority ought to be moved.'

Tricia felt very close to despair. 'What on earth is going to happen next?' she said to Paula. 'I'm not sure if I can cope with all this aggravation.'

'Look,' said Paula. 'I'm on duty now, you get off home and things will probably look a lot better tomorrow.'

*

Unfortunately, things didn't look any better the following day. The notices were still on the desk and the social worker from the Black Country had telephoned to say that she was coming that afternoon to pick up her client, Mrs Makin.

'What on earth does she mean?' said Tricia. 'Pick Mrs Makin up this afternoon? She's not a parcel; they can't just come and take her away without any preparation.'

However, all too sadly, they could. Mrs Makin's social worker, along with a representative from the local Social Services Department, arrived just after lunch. Mrs Makin's social worker, who introduced herself as Claire, said that she was extremely sorry but in view of the report from the local Social Services Department her Director had told her to move Mrs Makin straight away. Tricia asked Tim where Mrs Makin was at the moment and he replied that she was in her room having an after lunch nap.

She suggested to Claire that they go up and talk to Mrs Makin together, although she felt that it was really very unfair to be moving her without proper notice. They went upstairs and Tricia tapped gently on Mrs Makin's door. When they went in she wasn't on the bed but was sitting in the chair looking out of the window. She immediately recognised Claire and said, 'Hello, dear, I wasn't expecting a visit.'

Tricia said very gently, 'Claire has come to move you back to your own area.'

'But I don't want to go,' replied Mrs Makin. 'I'm quite happy here.'

Claire then said, 'Oh well, dear, we thought that you would like to move back to our area so that you would be near friends and relatives.'

'All my friends are here,' said Mrs Makin, 'and bugger my relatives, they haven't shown any interest in me for years.' She turned to Tricia and said, 'Do I have to go?'

Tricia explained to Mrs Makin that as she was partly financed by the Black Country authority they could make a decision as to where she lived.

Claire said, 'There's a nice new home opened in our town and we've got several vacancies, I'm sure you will love it there.'

Mrs Makin's eyes welled up with tears and Tricia felt that she couldn't bear it any longer. She left the room and asked Jean, one of the staff who was on duty, to go and help Mrs Makin and Claire to pack. She went to the office and rang Mr Khan, saying that she wasn't sure how much longer she could cope and explained about Mrs Makin. Mr Khan, although obviously disturbed, spoke to her soothingly and said, 'I will come over and see you in the morning.'

Claire knocked on the office door. 'We're ready to go now,' she said. 'I'm very sorry about this but the report from your authority suggested that the residents were not being properly cared for. Obviously, looking around and talking to Mrs Makin, it clearly isn't true but I'm afraid orders are orders.'

Tricia forced a smile and said, 'I understand.' Then she said goodbye to Mrs Makin, who was in tears. She waved them off and went back to her office. 'What exactly is going on?' she thought to herself.

There was a tragic irony to this particular move. Mrs Makin

had apparently been moved because of the suggestion that the residents of Hollytree House were not being properly cared for. Tricia heard a few weeks later that Mrs Makin had died as a result of peritonitis, which had been caused by a ruptured appendix. She could not help feeling that that would not have happened if Mrs Makin had not been moved.

Chapter Forty-Three

Mr Khan arrived on the Friday morning and it was clear to Tricia that he was not his usual calm and imperturbable self. He was accompanied by a very large and very well dressed lady, whom he introduced as Mrs Bacon.

'How are you, Tricia,' she said. 'I used to run this house for Mr Khan's mother.' She went on to say that although she was no longer in residential work she had heard on the grapevine about the current problems at Hollytree House and thought perhaps she could help.

Tricia wondered exactly which grapevine the news was being spread on and just why Mrs Bacon thought she could help.

'Perhaps we could have a look around,' Mrs Bacon suggested to Mr Khan.

He looked slightly uncomfortable and asked Tricia if it was alright for them to look around.

Tricia said, 'Why not, providing we do not upset the residents, there has been far too much upset in recent days.'

'Oh, by the way,' said Mrs Bacon. 'I meant to ask about the residents who died. Is there any question of a problem there?'

Tricia was furious. 'Bloody hell!' she thought. 'Now she thinks she's Miss Marple.' She endeavoured to remain as calm as possible for Mr Khan's sake and led the way into the sitting room. It was just before morning coffee and most of the residents were either sitting in there or in the music room. Mr Khan bade them all good morning and asked if any of them remembered Mrs Bacon.

Nobody responded and Mrs Bacon said, 'Well, it was thirteen years ago, I suppose most of the present clients have arrived since then.'

Tricia groaned inwardly and thought, 'Not clients, she'll be calling them customers next!' They continued their walk around the house and eventually finished up back in Tricia's office. Tricia said that she would go and get some coffee and made her way to the kitchen. She was delayed slightly because the cook wanted to talk about the following week's menu. When she got back to the office Mrs Bacon was leaning towards Mr Khan and talking in a very conspiratorial manner. She stopped when Tricia entered and there was an uneasy silence while Tricia handed round the coffee.

Mrs Bacon said that she was just telling Mr Khan how clean and tidy everywhere looked. 'Patronising cow,' thought Tricia, and she knew that there was no way that Mrs Bacon could be any help to her or to Hollytree House.

Then Mr Khan spoke. His voice was quiet and rather diffident. He said that Mrs Bacon had suggested that Tricia might like to take a holiday for about a month and she had offered to manage the house in Tricia's absence to see if she could sort out matters with Social Services.

For a moment Tricia was tempted. 'How nice to get away for a whole month and leave this dreadful situation behind me,' she thought. But then she thought, 'Oh yes, and after the month Mrs Bacon will calmly hand the reins back. I don't think so.'

'Well thank you,' she said to Mr Khan, 'but I cannot desert the residents now.'

Mrs Bacon interjected saying, 'I assure you the residents will be in very good hands.' Tricia turned to Mrs Bacon and asked what made her think she could sort things out with Social Services. Mrs Bacon said that she and Mr Slighe had once been fellow students on an in-service course and had been really good friends. Her smile seemed to imply that they had been considerably more that just good friends.

'Alright,' said Tricia, 'why don't you talk to Mr Slighe first and then we can discuss the next step.'

Mr Khan looked relieved and said he thought that was a good suggestion. Mrs Bacon did not look particularly happy but said, 'I will contact James first thing on Monday and then come back to you.'

Tricia showed them out and thought, 'What comes next?

What came next was the Ken Pratt problem. He came on duty in the afternoon and it was to be his weekend on. It was very obvious that relationships between him and the residents were very strained. He was due to leave on Monday 31st and Tricia thought it would save embarrassment both for him and the residents if he left on Friday evening and had the weekend off. Little did she realise that even a small gesture like that could have repercussions. In the event Pratt left promptly at nine o'clock without saying goodbye to anybody.

CHAPTER FORTY-FOUR

It proved to be a quiet and pleasant weekend. Because she had given Pratt the weekend off Tricia felt that she ought to be around, and on Saturday, she, Paula and Bridie were on duty. On Sunday Tricia asked her husband Robbie to spend the day at Hollytree House with her, where Paula and June were now on duty. In the afternoon she and Robbie took eight of the residents for a drive and they had afternoon tea in a large garden centre. Such places were always popular with the residents, who wandered round looking at plants and pets and all the other things that garden centres now seemed to sell.

After dinner Paula said, 'You do look very tired, Tricia. The residents are all relaxed and settled, why don't you and Robbie go home and have an early night?'

Tricia was very tired and reluctantly agreed to leave just after seven-thirty, leaving Paula and June on duty until the night staff arrived at nine p.m. As they drove home they passed a pub where Robbie occasionally played pool and he asked Tricia if she would mind if they stopped for a quick drink so that he could check the fixture list. They sat quietly in the corner of the comfortable warm pub, Tricia drinking a gin and tonic and Robbie a pint of beer.

He disappeared for a few minutes to talk to some of his fellow pool players and Tricia sat there almost falling asleep. When Robbie reappeared she asked if he would mind if they went home as she was very tired. Robbie said, 'Of course darling,' and they finished their journey.

They sat in front of the television, although Tricia had very little idea about what they were watching. For some reason she had a very uncomfortable feeling, but didn't know why. Just after nine o'clock the telephone rang. Robbie answered and then said, 'It's Paula for you.' Tricia took the telephone with a feeling of disaster and said hello. At the other end Paula burst into tears and told Tricia that at eight o'clock three inspectors had turned up.

'On a Sunday evening?' gasped Tricia. 'Why didn't you contact me straight away.'

'I would have done,' said Paula, 'but while the two women snooped around, Mr Slighe sat in the office, and I obviously couldn't use the telephone. He asked to see the staff rota and made a great fuss because there was no man on duty and there was only June and me here. They left after an hour. Slighe had a face like thunder and said we would be receiving a letter before the week was out.'

'Well,' said Tricia, 'there's nothing more we can do now, I will see you in the morning.'

Paula again apologised and Tricia tried to reassure her. They eventually made their goodbyes.

Tricia turned to Robbie and explained the situation. She said that she didn't understand why they had visited on a Sunday evening and how could they have known that there might be a staff problem.

'Look,' said Robbie. 'The residents were settled and we're only talking about less than two hours.'

Tricia said that that was enough for someone like Slighe and he needed no excuse to cause trouble. Robbie suggested that he would heat up some milk for a supper drink and that they should then go to bed. Tricia agreed but said that there was very little likelihood of her sleeping.

CHAPTER FORTY-FIVE

Later that week Reuben Jones called a meeting of what he was now calling 'the right to buy consortium'. He explained that he wanted the meeting to be at his house rather than his office because of the continued need for secrecy. He invited Jack Smith and James Slighe for lunch on the Thursday; he chose that day because his wife always went out to an art appreciation group in the afternoon. After a very pleasant lunch of chicken casserole followed by roasted pears in a caramel sauce he thanked his wife and said, 'You get off to your meeting, dear, I will arrange coffee for our guests.'

They took their coffee into the conservatory and Reuben also brought in a very decent cognac, which he offered to his fellow conspirators. He then asked both of them how matters were proceeding. Jack Smith told them that for his part everything was going very smoothly, the exchange of houses had taken place and he thought that Mr Khan had been very satisfied with the arrangement. 'Unfortunately,' he said with a chuckle, 'I hear from my manager that there are some problems at Hollytree House and that the manager there maybe on the verge of resigning.'

Slighe said that he wouldn't be at all surprised if that happened as he and his colleagues had been giving them a very hard time. Smith said that he'd heard about this and he was very glad that the Haven wasn't the target.

'What puzzles me,' said Reuben Jones, addressing Slighe,

'is how you get your staff to co-operate without them knowing what the reasons are for the campaign of harassment?'

'Oh I've got them well trained,' said Slighe with a smirk. 'If I say "jump" they say "how high, Mr Slighe?"'

'Well I can understand that with the women,' said Jones, 'because presumably they were carefully handpicked by you, but what about your deputy, surely he smells a rat?'

'Oh no,' said Slighe, 'I've led him to believe that I may be moving on soon and that I'm grooming him to take over. 'Mind you,' he added, 'with the best part of a million pounds I may go and live in France.'

Jack Smith then asked Jones if he'd made any progress. 'Well I've come to an unofficial gentleman's agreement with my developer friend,' he replied. 'He wants the land sale finalised by the end of March and he is willing to pay three and a quarter million pounds for it. It's then up to us how much we agree with Khan.'

Jack Smith said, 'From what I hear he's getting very nervous and he will probably settle for half a million pounds when James and his minions have finished.'

Slighe then said he thought he could have the closure order in place within twenty-eight days, about the first week in March.

'Well, it shouldn't take long to arrange a takeover,' said Jack Smith. 'I'll offer to buy Khan out as soon as the closure order is published. I'm sure you can push the legal bits through, Reuben.'

Jones replied that the land registry may take some time but once his friend had the signed contract he would be quite happy.

'Well, that seems to be all for now,' said Slighe. 'I'll be off. Remember to keep in touch only with the mobiles, no calls to my office please.' With that he and Smith made their farewells and Reuben Jones poured himself another large cognac.

Chapter Forty-six

Two things happened to Tricia that week, one of which caused her wry amusement and the other drove her into the depths of despair. She hadn't heard from Mrs Bacon on Monday so on Tuesday she phoned Mr Khan and asked if he had heard anything. Mr Khan said that he too had not heard but he would contact Mrs Bacon and ask her to get in touch with Tricia. On Tuesday afternoon Mrs Bacon telephoned Tricia, who was interested that her voice sounded much less confident and bombastic.

She asked Mrs Bacon whether she had spoken to James Slighe and after some hesitation she admitted that she had. She told Tricia that she had said she was thinking about temporarily taking over Hollytree House and asked whether this would make any difference to James Slighe's plans. She was discomfited by the fact that Slighe had laughed out loud and said he didn't care if the Prime Minister's wife was taking over Hollytree House; it was still going to close. Mrs Bacon went on to say that under the circumstances she felt she could no longer offer her services. Tricia replied that she was sorry to hear that but she would soldier on. She could not resist a small smile as she put the telephone down. 'Just what the pompous cow deserved,' she thought.

The second incident was a letter, which arrived on Thursday from James Slighe. In it he accused her of having a staff rota which was not accurate and that there had been a number of other matters during Sunday's visit which would be included in the next batch of notices. The letter went on to say that in his opinion there was very little alternative but for him to issue a closure order on Hollytree House as the residents were definitely at risk.

Tricia called Tim and Paula into the office and read the letter to them. Her despair was increased when Paula said that she had been discussing the problems with her husband and they felt that her continued involvement at Hollytree House was likely to damage her professional career. She said that she was very keen to stay in social work and under the circumstances she felt that she had to give Tricia a month's notice. Tricia was very upset but said that she did understand Paula's point of view and under the circumstances felt that she would have to accept the resignation, although she was very sad because she and Paula had worked happily together for six years.

Tricia turned to Tim and said, 'How about you, Tim?'

He replied, 'Don't worry about me, boss, I'll be here as long as you need me.'

Tricia thanked him but could not help feeling that Hollytree House was falling down around her ears.

CHAPTER FORTY-SEVEN

On Friday morning the Major knocked on Tricia's office door and asked her if there had been any further developments. Tricia told him that there had been and it looked increasingly likely that Hollytree House might have to close. 'Over my dead body,' said the Major, and striding off into the sitting room he called for a meeting of the liar dice team and the bridge group. He suggested that they took their coffee into the music room so that they could discuss the situation.

When they were all seated he brought them up to date as far as he could and told them that Hollytree House was in grave danger of closing. There was a heated discussion and then Vic suggested that they ought to establish a proper committee and develop a realistic fighting fund.

'Good idea,' said Jerry. 'We should at least show that we are capable of being properly organised.'

'We must elect a chairman or a chairperson,' interjected Harriet.

Willy said that she would propose the Major as chairman but the Major declined this and said that his role would be better acting as the go-between with Tricia. 'In any case,' he went on, 'you've all been here a lot longer than I have.'

After further discussion it was decided that Jerry should be Chairman and Harriet would be the Vice Chair. They then went on to consider whether any of the other residents should be involved at this stage. Since the deaths of Old Tom and

Mrs Hargreaves there were now seventeen residents, but the Major pointed out that Tricia did not want the older or more disturbed residents to be upset.

Jerry said that he understood that but he thought that the more residents that were involved the stronger the committee would be. More discussions followed and it was agreed that Mrs Harrington-Ford and her friend, Milly, were pretty sturdy characters and should be invited to join them.

Glyn said that Peter Banks would be useful too. 'He's an ex policeman,' he added. Nobody was quite sure how relevant that was but it was agreed that Peter and another male resident, Bill Colley, should also be invited.

'That gives us a full cricket team and a reserve,' said Jerry jokingly but nobody laughed.

Joyce said, 'About the fighting fund, do you think we might get a grant from the Lottery people?'

'No chance,' said Jerry, 'it's a damn farce. The pathetic people who run it take far too much for their own salaries for a start.'

'Yes,' added Vic, 'and in their attempts to demonstrate their political correctness they make the most ludicrous awards to all kinds of weird causes.'

'Well,' said Poppy, who was sitting on the settee holding Vic's hand, 'we will obviously have to look elsewhere.' And they all looked automatically at the Major.

It was agreed that all twelve of them would meet on Sunday afternoon when the oldest residents would be having a nap. After the meeting broke up the Major went to Tricia's office and told her that they had formed a committee which would stop Hollytree House from closing. Tricia responded with a wan smile and said she was sure that that would help.

Chapter Forty-Eight

There were lots of individual discussions throughout the whole of Saturday. In the afternoon the Major asked to be excused because he wanted to watch the television in his room. He explained that he needed to watch the racing very carefully as he was in the process of drawing up his short list for the Cheltenham Festival.

*

On Friday evening Tim had volunteered to cover the weekend and Andy offered to join him. He told Tricia that he knew he was not officially care staff but that he did know and like the residents. Tricia was very touched and said, 'Thank you, Andy. I know the residents like you and I really must get away for a couple of days.' She went on to say that Robbie, her husband, was going to drive her down to Bournemouth for a brief weekend break. Tim remarked that as Jean and Edna were on duty on Saturday and June and Bridie would be on duty on Sunday, Tricia could be sure that the home would be in safe hands. He added that even if the inspectors did call they wouldn't be able to find any fault with the staffing arrangements.

On Sunday afternoon the committee convened in the sitting room and welcomed their four new members. Three of the older residents had gone to their rooms and Andy volunteered to take the other two for a short ride. Harriet reported that she had spoken to her friend, the retired solicitor, who had told her that if a residential home is registered with the local authority, it could be closed down if that authority felt it was not being run in a satisfactory manner.

'That's the irony of the situation,' said the Major. 'As you know, I spent a short time at the Haven and Hollytree House is vastly superior.'

Glyn said that he thought there must be some hidden agenda because until very recently there hadn't been any problems and they all agreed that it was a lovely place to live.

Jerry asked Harriet what the position was if the home was not registered. 'Supposing we set ourselves up as a commune,' he said. Vic then pointed out that Mr Khan ran the home as a business and he would be very unlikely just to hand it over to them.

After further discussion it was decided that there were only two viable options: One, that they must fight the local authority and resist any attempt to close the home, or secondly, that they created a commune and did not have to register as a home for the elderly. It was agreed that the first option would be extremely difficult, although Jerry said that they should at least get the local Member of Parliament involved.

'Fat lot of good that will be,' said Glyn. 'Politicians are not interested in the likes of us, and the present Government is a pathetic collection of losers. Why, the Deputy Prime Minister would never have got a place in any crew I have ever served in.'

'What about local councillors then?' asked Harriet.

'Even worse,' said Jerry. 'They're not going to oppose their own officials.'

'Well, why do people become councillors?' said Willy.

'Self-glorification is the quick answer,' said Vic. 'They

usually are getting nowhere in their day jobs and they think that being a councillor will make them important.'

'Ah yes,' said Willy, 'like Eric Pollard in *Emmerdale*.'

'Well, that's just fiction,' said Vic, 'but it's probably not that far from the truth.'

The Major said, 'I don't want to stop this fascinating discussion but I think that we should consider the second option. It may be very expensive to create a commune but the home would be free of bureaucracy and red tape forever.'

At that point Tim came in and said, 'Excuse me interrupting but we've got you a special tea ready.'

'That's alright,' said Jerry. 'We have finished and we will meet again on Wednesday.'

Chapter Forty-Nine

After lunch on Monday Tricia came back from her short break looking much less tired and feeling ready to cope with Slighe's next step. However, that morning James Slighe had called his staff together to develop his plans for the closure order. He told them that he was issuing further notices and Mr Heap asked what these were. Slighe ticked them off on the fingers of his hand: 'Firstly, despite our request, they have not fenced the pool properly; secondly, they do not have sufficient staff on duty at the weekends and the staff rota is inaccurate; thirdly, a member of staff or a resident committed a serious assault on another resident, and fourthly, it appears that they are employing an ex criminal on their staff.

He went on to explain that Miss Burley had discovered that Tim Jones had been in prison for a drug offence. Mr Heap said, 'But we've known about that for a long time and it was only a very minor offence, which really had no bearing on the residents.'

'That's not the point,' said Slighe. 'In order to get a closure order we need as much ammunition as possible. For example, two of the residents have recently died; this could easily be due to neglect.'

Mrs Dennison, who was the newest inspector, said rather diffidently that she didn't understand what was going on at Hollytree House because she had known Tricia Beasley for several years and had always rated her very highly. James

Slighe was not amused and said abruptly that that comment just indicated how new Mrs Dennison was to the job and how much she still had to learn. Mrs Dennison flushed and said nothing further.

James Slighe then went on to say that after the meeting he would go to the Director of Social Services and ask him to convene a meeting with a view to closure. 'Who will attend the meeting?' asked his deputy, Mr Heap. Slighe explained that the Director would chair the meeting and that three inspectors – himself, Mr Heap and Miss Burley – would be present. 'Hollytree House will have to be represented by the owner, Mr Khan, and the Manager, Mrs Beasley. They can also bring along a solicitor,' he said, 'and we can get one of the tame solicitors from the legal department.' He said that they were pretty useless, which was why they were not in private practice, but they could sit there and look the part. 'In any event,' he went on, 'we have a completely watertight case so solicitors will not need to be involved.'

Mrs Burley then asked if Mr Slighe was sure that the Director would be co-operative. Slighe replied that as he'd said before, the Director wasn't the brightest star in the firmament and in any case was moving towards retirement.

Mrs Dennison thought, 'Mr Slighe seems to think he's cleverer than anybody else,' and she wondered whether perhaps she herself was in the right job.

After Slighe closed the meeting he sat at his desk with his hands behind his head and wondered whether he should think very seriously about retiring. He knew that if he took early retirement he would still get a reasonable pension and he would have almost a million pounds as his share of the forced sale. He thought about the timing and decided that it would be a good idea if he gave three months' notice now in case there was any fallout. He smiled to himself and thought, 'It's the opportunity of a lifetime.'

Chapter Fifty

Early in February, Jack Smith telephoned Mr Khan and asked if they could meet. They arranged to meet at Mr Khan's shop and although the meeting was scheduled for ten-thirty Jack Smith didn't turn up until just before lunch. He told Mr Khan that he was continuing to hear that Hollytree House was having problems and he wondered whether he could help.

Mr Khan said that he was totally bewildered; he had no idea why Social Services were harassing Hollytree House and he asked Jack Smith if they were having problems at the Haven. Jack replied that they weren't having problems at the Haven and he thought it was very unfair that Mr Khan was having so much trouble. He said that he couldn't help wondering whether there was some kind of racial element involved. 'Surely not,' said Mr Khan, 'my mother and I have never had any trouble before. I am quite sure that is not the reason.' He then went on to say that perhaps it was time that he returned to Pakistan. He explained that his brother-in-law had built a very nice property development business in Islamabad and he had asked Mr Khan to join him.

'Well why not?' said Jack Smith. 'Perhaps it would be the best solution.' He then went on to say that even as they had sat there talking, he had had an idea. 'Supposing I buy you out,' he suggested.

Mr Khan was taken aback and then said, 'But what good

is it to you if the powers that be are determined to close it down?'

Smith replied that he was willing to take a chance and went on to say that if the two homes were combined again perhaps Social Services would drop their action.

Mr Khan then asked, 'What kind of money are we talking about?'

Jack Smith pretended to think for a moment and then said, 'How about four hundred thousand pounds?'

Mr Khan was taken aback and said that surely the building and grounds alone were worth more than that.

'Ah,' said Jack Smith, 'but you've always said that your mother wanted you to keep it open.'

Mr Khan replied, 'That is very true but I think half a million would be a fairer price.'

Jack Smith replied that he had a cash flow problem at the moment. '…But we, I mean I, could probably raise four hundred and fifty thousand if you would meet us half way.'

Mr Khan, who was nobody's fool, noticed the slip and it only increased his suspicions.

'Yes, well I'll think about it,' he said. 'But I really would like to get to the bottom of the mystery.'

Jack Smith promised that he would make some enquiries and let Mr Khan know if he learned anything that was relevant and then took his leave. Later that day he telephoned Reuben Jones and told him that he thought they had Mr Khan firmly on the hook.

Chapter Fifty-One

Monday the 14th of February was St Valentines Day, and both Mr Khan and Tricia received a fat brown envelope by recorded delivery. Tricia knew before she opened it what it would probably contain, and she also knew that James Slighe had deliberately chosen this particular day for the delivery. When she opened the envelope she found that it contained further notices and a letter which informed her and Mr Khan that a meeting had been called for the 28th of February in the Social Services office. The letter went on to say that the meeting would consider the withdrawal of the registration for Hollytree House and that Mr Khan and Tricia should both attend. It also stated that if they wished to bring their solicitor this would be acceptable.

Mr Khan was at Hollytree House by ten o'clock and he was clearly very upset. He asked Tricia about the notices and she explained that they were really a further collection of trumped-up charges. Mr Khan said that they would of course have to go to the meeting but the way things looked at present caused him to have little hope that they would be able to prevent the closure. He went on to say that from what he'd heard from other proprietors these meetings were little more than kangaroo courts. 'Apart from us everyone else is employed by Social Services and there will be no outside impartial adjudicator. The meetings are a farce and a travesty of justice,' he concluded.

Tricia asked whether they would be taking a solicitor to the meeting. Mr Khan replied that he supposed they would have to but the problem would be to get someone who would be any use. He said that he hated to generalise but most of the solicitors he had encountered were either incompetent or dishonest and in some cases both.

Tricia felt near to tears but tried very hard to control herself. She went on to say that it was the residents she felt most sympathy for because they would be dispersed and placed wherever there was a vacancy, regardless of whether it would be suitable or not. 'Most of them have become very good friends,' she said, 'and I really don't know how some of them will cope if they are moved.' Mr. Khan then told her of Jack Smith's offer. Tricia said that there was no way she would ever trust Jack Smith and she couldn't help feeling that he was somehow mixed up in the whole messy business.

'I agree,' said Mr Khan, 'but what else can I do, it looks like I'm between a rock and a hard place.' He left, shaking his head and promising to be in touch before the 28th.

Tricia then called her staff together and told them about the meeting and the possible outcome. Paula seemed to have already switched off and took very little interest but Tim and Andy were very angry and said that they would support Tricia in whatever action she thought was best. Bridie said that she was ever so sorry but she thought that now she would really make an effort to take her sons back to Ireland. Lucy said that she would stay at Hollytree House as long as Tricia needed her, and she was supported in this by June and Mrs Halliday. Before Tricia closed the meeting she reminded the staff to be as cautious and gentle as they could with the residents. 'For what it's worth,' she said 'they have formed a committee, bless them, but I don't know whether that will be a help or a hindrance.'

CHAPTER FIFTY-TWO

Later that week Hollytree House was visited by Mrs Stevens. She was one of the senior administrative officers in the Social Services Department and was responsible for the placement of a number of residents in the home. She asked if she could address the residents in the coffee break and Tricia queried whether it was necessary for her to speak to all the residents at this stage. Mrs Stevens was most insistent and said that she and her colleagues believed it was time that all the residents knew the full situation.

Tricia very reluctantly took her into the sitting room where all the residents were sitting round drinking their morning coffee. She introduced Mrs Stevens, who then spoke at some length about the anxieties that the Social Services Department felt and the possibility that the home could be closed down. The first response was a stony silence and many of the residents just sat and glared at this woman who was interrupting their coffee break.

Eventually the Major said, 'But the home hasn't closed yet and I really don't think you should come here upsetting my friends.'

Mrs Stevens responded that as far as she was concerned the home would be closing in the very near future and she would be coming to move three of the residents in the following week.

After she had left most of the residents were furious. Jerry said, 'What a bloody arrogant woman, having the nerve to come here patronising us.'

Glyn said that he thought her sour face was probably due to a bad case of haemorrhoids and the Major said, 'Well piles or no piles, she's not going to close this home down.'

Tricia tried to calm the residents down and said that there was still no confirmation that Hollytree House would close, however she thought it was only fair to tell them about the meeting which was to be held at the end of the month. At this meeting, she explained the future of the home would be discussed. She urged them not to get too distressed as she believed something would turn up. 'Just call me Mrs Micawber,' she joked but then quickly left the room in case she burst into tears.

At lunchtime Jerry called a meeting of the committee and when they gathered in the music room he said it was time that they got their act together and did something as quickly as possible. Willy said that they should make some posters and start parading outside but the Major said that they should not take any overt action without discussing it first with Tricia and the staff. He went on to say that it looked as if the Social Services Department were determined to close the home down and he still believed that the commune idea was the most likely course of action.

He explained that he was still working on the financial plan and Jerry asked if he could come up with the plan by the end of the month. It was agreed that once the meeting Tricia had told them about had taken place matters would escalate very fast. The Major replied that he would do his very best and the meeting closed. After the meeting the Major went to see Tricia and she very sadly confirmed that if the meeting decided to close the home then they would only have twenty-eight days' notice.

Chapter Fifty-Three

The following Monday, Mrs Stevens telephoned and said that she and two social workers would be coming that afternoon to move three of the residents. When Tricia queried why she was acting at such short notice and before any confirmation of the closure, Mrs Stevens replied that she thought the residents were at risk. When she and her colleagues arrived in the afternoon she said that she was moving Mrs Bevan, Mrs Harrison and Mr James to a home about twenty-five miles away. She said that they were all going to the same home and would therefore be together. Tricia knew the home in question and had a very low opinion of it and she protested that she thought such a hurried move was totally unnecessary. Mrs Stevens, however, said that she was not prepared to argue; the Council paid the bills and the Council decided where they should live.

Tricia went to find June and Tim and asked them to help the social workers pack up the belongings of the unfortunate three. The other residents were perturbed at the sudden influx of Social Services staff and asked the Major to find out from Tricia exactly what was happening. She explained that it was a repeat of the action a few weeks earlier when the social worker came to move Mrs Makin. The Major reported back to the other residents and a heavy feeling of gloom and despondency settled over the sitting room like a black cloud.

A number of the ladies were very near to tears and Glyn and Vic said they would barricade the front door so that the social workers could not take their friends away. The Major said that he thought this would be a pointless exercise and would only increase the distress of the three residents who were leaving. Instead most of them gathered in the hall and when Mrs Bevan, Mrs Harrison and Mr James came downstairs they were greeted with lots of hugs and handshakes and wishes of good luck. Mrs Bevan was openly crying but Mrs Harrison and Mr James simply looked bewildered and quite clearly were not at all sure as to what was going on.

Tricia was upset when she heard one of the social workers whisper to Mr James, 'Don't worry, dear, we're just going for a little ride.'

'They can't even be honest now,' she thought.

As the group left the other residents followed them into the garden and waved and shouted or simply burst into tears themselves. It was one of the most distressing moments of Tricia's career and she thought, 'If this is bad, how on earth am I going to cope if everybody has to move.' She simply could not understand how this situation had arisen. Both she and the staff had always tried very hard to run a caring home and for some reason somebody was setting out to destroy it.

Chapter Fifty-Four

There were now only fourteen residents left and the meeting in the Social Services Department was in one week's time. Apart from the committee of twelve there were two very elderly and rather frail residents, both of whom were completely self-financing through the medium of family trusts. Mrs Robertson and Miss Ellis had both been at Hollytree House since before Tricia became manager. She decided that she would contact the Trustees in both cases and put them honestly in the picture. She made a note to contact the responsible Trustees the following morning.

On Wednesday afternoon Jerry called a meeting of the committee. He told them that they were running out of time and that they must now get down to the firm details of the commune plan. He pointed out that it was not simply a matter of buying the house from Mr Khan and Harriet asked him to explain this further. He said that in addition to the purchase cost, they would need enough money to run the commune for at least ten years because obviously they would get no support from the local authority.

The running costs would include employing some staff and general expenses such as heat, light and food. He and the Major had done some figures and calculated that they would need fifty thousand a year in addition to the normal individual contributions. Vic then said that it was quite clear that they would need at least a million pounds overall, and he asked where on earth they were going to get a sum like that. Jerry replied that it would mean everyone contributing about eighty thousand pounds each.

When he said this there were a number of groans and gasps and after a frantic discussion it was apparent that such a sum would be beyond most of the residents. Willy then joined in and asked about the Major's plan and the Major replied by saying that for many years he had been trying to find an accumulator for the four main races at the Cheltenham National Hunt Festival. Willy voiced what many of the others would be thinking when she said that they knew the Major was good at selecting horses but surely if he had never accomplished the accumulator before it was unlikely that he could do it now. The Major smiled and said, 'But I have never had this kind of incentive before.' He then asked if they could have a meeting on Saturday when he would finalise his plans.

Chapter Fifty-Five

The remainder of the week seemed to pass very quickly. On Saturday morning the home was visited by more relatives than Tricia could ever remember seeing before. They were all very concerned and Tricia learned that James Slighe had written to all of them saying that there was to be a meeting on the 28th of February to discuss the possibility of the home being closed. Tricia tried to stay as calm as possible and reassure the relatives that everything was running normally and the welfare of the residents was still paramount. The residents themselves told their visitors quite firmly that they were very happy at Hollytree House and had no intention of being moved.

Tricia had had a good response from the Trustees concerned with Mrs Robertson and Miss Ellis and was in some strange way beginning to feel a little more confident about the future. The Major assured her that the residents had the situation well in hand and they were sure that Hollytree House was going to stay open. He asked Tricia to excuse him if he didn't give any more details at this point but he would prefer the committee to finalise their plans before divulging exactly what they were. The visitors gradually dispersed and by lunchtime there were just the fourteen residents plus June, Tim and Tricia. Tim produced three bottles of wine which he said were left over from the New Year celebrations and they all drank a toast to the future of Hollytree House.

In the afternoon the committee met and the Major outlined

his plan. He said that there were four races at the Cheltenham Festival, which he wanted to win. He was absolutely certain that a horse called Istabraq would win the Champion Hurdle; it had won the race in the two previous years and he was sure it would succeed for the third time. Unfortunately the price would be very short but he was going to negotiate with the local bookmakers. He then went on to say that the Queen Mother Champion Chase would very likely be won by a horse called Edredon Bleu, a name which was translated as the Blue Bedspread. The third leg was the Cheltenham Gold Cup, and by one of these strange quirks of fate the horse he thought would win was called Looks Like Trouble.

'Well,' said Harriet, 'that's three horses. What about the fourth?'

'Ah,' said the Major, 'the fourth race is called the Triumph Hurdle and it is for four-year-olds only; it is probably the hardest race in which to forecast the winner.' He then went on to admit that he could not do so with a great deal of confidence.

Glyn said, 'Not much use then, having three winners if we can't find the fourth.'

The Major replied that perhaps they would have to rely on beginner's luck and see if one of the ladies had a hunch. He proposed to read out the list of entries for the Triumph Hurdle and see if anyone had an inspiration. He read slowly through the list, which was in alphabetical order, and as he got to the bottom he named a horse called Snowdrop. Willy gave a shriek and said, 'I saw one this morning by the gate, the first this year and that's obviously a good omen.'

After some debate, the Major informed the group that Snowdrop was actually one of the most fancied horses. It was a French-trained horse, trained by a man called François Doumen. Glyn said, 'Oh well, that's probably put the mockers on it then. You don't get many 'Frog' horses winning over

A MAJOR MIRACLE

here.' However, after further discussion it was agreed that Snowdrop would be their selection.

The Major then went on to explain that in order to win over a million pounds they would need a very substantial outlay and when he was asked by Harriet exactly what he meant by substantial he said that if all twelve of them put in two hundred pounds he would divide the bet between two bookmakers and negotiate the best possible prices. He felt fairly confident that if he explained the situation to the managers of the betting offices they would be sympathetic and fair. Again there was some heated discussion with a number of people questioning whether they should risk losing two hundred pounds, but Jerry emphasised that it was a very small risk compared with the chance of winning over a million pounds and securing the future of Hollytree House. Finally it was agreed that everyone would obtain two hundred pounds and give it to the Major on the following Wednesday.

Chapter Fifty-Six

On Friday the 25th of February James Slighe convened a hasty meeting of his staff. He said to them, 'As you know we have the registration meeting on Monday.' He then told them that they would descend on Hollytree House on Sunday afternoon. 'You never know,' he went on, 'an unexpected visit might just shock them into making mistakes and give us more ammunition for Monday. Mr Heap, Miss Burley and I should be enough,' he said, with one of his recognisable sneers.

Mrs Dennison thought this was a disgusting plan and quite unnecessary. She resolved to do something about it.

On Friday evening Tricia received a call from someone who sounded vaguely familiar but did not give their name.

'They are planning a visit for two o'clock on Sunday,' the voice said, and then the telephone line went dead. Tricia sat looking at the telephone for a few minutes and then went in search of the staff that were on duty. Tim was sitting in the kitchen talking to Andy and June; Andy had called in on his way past just to see if everything was alright. Tricia blurted out the information from the telephone call and for a moment there was a stunned silence.

'What a lousy trick,' said Tim. 'Is there nothing that Slighe wouldn't stoop to?'

'The problem is,' said Tricia, 'what do we do?'

Andy smiled and said, 'Supposing they couldn't get in.'

'What do you mean,' said Tim.

A MAJOR MIRACLE

Andy said, 'Well, if the staff took the residents out for the afternoon I could amuse myself by stalling them. I could tell them that I could not let them into the house without permission from Tricia or Mr Khan and I couldn't contact them.'

'Yes,' Tricia responded, 'we could go out after lunch and have tea somewhere, not getting back until after dark.'

'Great idea,' said Tim.

Tricia asked Andy if he would be able to cope. 'I will really enjoy it,' said Andy with a laugh.

*

At one thirty on Sunday afternoon, following an early lunch, all the residents plus Tricia, Tim and Paula climbed into the minibus and Tricia's car. Andy waved them off with a broad grin and proceeded to trim one of the hedges. Promptly at two o'clock three cars roared up the drive, each car containing just the driver. All three inspectors got out and assembled on the front step, totally ignoring Andy. Slighe first of all rang the bell and, getting no response, hammered on the door. There was still no response so he walked over to Andy and said very rudely, 'Where is everyone?'

Andy kept a straight face and said, 'If you mean Mrs Beasley and the residents, they have gone out for a ride.'

Well you'd better let us in then,' responded Slighe aggressively.

'Oh I couldn't do that,' said Andy. 'Not without permission from Mrs Beasley or Mr Khan.'

'Well telephone them and get permission,' snarled Slighe, who was obviously close to losing his temper.

'I'm only the gardener,' said Andy, 'and I don't have their numbers.'

'Well what time will they be back?' Slighe asked.

'Well usually they go for about two hours,' Andy replied.

'Right,' said Slighe, 'we'll wait,' and the three inspectors got back into one car.

After a while Andy went down to his shed and had a cup of tea from a flask he had prepared earlier. At three-thirty Slighe approached him again and said, 'There's still no sign of them'.

'Ah, I've just remembered,' said Andy. 'They said they may have tea out.'

By five o'clock it was getting quite dark and Slighe said to his two companions, 'This is a complete waste of time, we may as well call it a day.'

Andy had a broad grin as he watched them drive off and half an hour later he greeted Tricia and the residents on their return. When he told them what had transpired, for once they all had something to smile about.

Chapter Fifty-Seven

Monday morning arrived and Tricia met Mr Khan in the offices of the Social Services Department. He was accompanied by a fresh-faced young man whom he introduced as Mr Healey, his solicitor. While they were sitting in the waiting area the local authority solicitor came in and said good morning, he was obviously on first name terms with Mr Healey. This did not fill Tricia with a lot of optimism. After about twenty minutes they were called into a large room with a very long table. At one end sat the Director of Social Services flanked on his right by James Slighe and two of his minions, and on his left by the solicitor and someone who was obviously a clerical officer, there to make notes. Mr Khan, Mr Healey and Tricia sat at the opposite end of the table.

The Director turned to James Slighe and asked him to outline the purpose of the meeting. Slighe said that as a result of a number of unsatisfactory inspections he and his staff felt that Hollytree House was an unsuitable home and even worse he thought that the residents were at risk. He referred the Director to the reports in front of him and copies were passed down to Mr Khan and Tricia. Tricia was not surprised to see that it listed all the faults, real and imaginary, and painted a very damning, but totally untrue, picture of Hollytree House.

James Slighe explained that he and his staff had visited on a number of occasions and felt very strongly that the home should have its registration removed.

The Director did not seem to be taking a vast amount of interest and kept looking out of the window.

The local authority solicitor asked James Slighe a number of questions and then Mr Khan was asked if he or his solicitor had anything to say. Tricia was disappointed but not surprised when neither Mr Khan nor Mr Healey made any particular protests.

She was then asked if she had anything to say and she responded quite firmly by saying that most of the allegations in the report were either untrue or blown out of proportion. She felt that the whole process was a total waste of time because it was quite clear what the outcome would be. 'Nevertheless,' she continued, 'I believe that it is not fair on the residents who are perfectly happy in Hollytree House. Closing down the home is neither necessary nor just.'

Slighe interrupted. 'With respect, Mrs Beasley, it is our job to decide what is in the best interests of the residents.'

Tricia could have said more but realised that she would be wasting her breath.

After a few more minutes of discussion James Slighe asked Mr Khan if he and his party would wait outside whilst the panel deliberated. They sat in the waiting area for something like half an hour and saw coffee being taken into the meeting room and occasionally heard laughter.

Mr Khan said, 'It's just as I expected, a damn kangaroo court. We have no chance.'

James Slighe then came to the door and asked them if they would go back into the room.

They sat themselves in their original places and the Director said, 'Well I'm very sorry to have to tell you that the panel have agreed that the registration for Hollytree House should be withdrawn. Under the circumstances we would expect the home to close by the end of March. You can, of course, appeal,' he said, but he said it in such a way it was clear any appeal would be bound to fail.

James Slighe then spoke and said how sorry he was that the panel had to reach such a conclusion but he would like to thank Mrs Beasley for her co-operation.

'Bloody hypocrite,' thought Tricia, but felt that she could not safely respond without losing her temper.

The three of them left the room and Tricia thought what a waste of space the solicitor was. He shook hands with Mr Khan and said he was very sorry but if Mr Khan wanted to appeal he would be prepared to help. 'I don't think so,' said Mr Khan. 'It was all such a disgraceful charade.'

He and Tricia then made their way back to Hollytree House and whilst they were sitting in Tricia's office the Major knocked on the door. He asked whether it would be possible for him and his colleague, Jerry, to have a word with Mr Khan. Tricia looked at Mr Khan, who had a very defeated air about him, and suggested that he should come back later in the week and talk to the Major and Jerry. He agreed to do this and an appointment was made for Thursday.

Chapter Fifty-Eight

On Wednesday morning the Major collected two hundred pounds from every member of the committee. He was a bit uneasy about carrying that amount of cash with him so he asked Jerry if he would accompany him to the bookmakers. His plan was to place a bet with each of the two main bookmakers in the town and it was simplified by the fact that he knew the managers and they in turn had known the Major for some time. He explained to Jerry that the best price he could get for the horse in the Champion Hurdle, which was Istabraq, was at odds of eleven to ten on so he proposed to start each accumulator with an eleven hundred pound bet as the Champion Hurdle was the first race of the accumulator.

Jerry said, 'Well I'm not incredibly good at arithmetic but it seems to me that that would be a total of two thousand, two hundred pounds, and we have collected two thousand, four hundred pounds.'

'That's right,' the Major replied. He then went on to say that he intended to keep two hundred pounds back so that they could have a party whether they won or lost. Jerry thought this was a splendid idea and they went into the first bookmakers.

The Major asked to see the manager and they went to one end of the counter where they would not be overheard by the other people in the betting office. After some discussion and

A MAJOR MIRACLE

an explanation by the Major it was agreed that they would back the first horse at odds of eleven to ten on, the second horse, Edredon Bleu, at odds of four to one against, the third horse, Snowdrop, would be at odds of eight to one, and the fourth horse, Looks Like Trouble, would be at five to one. The manager pointed out that he was being as helpful as possible because both Edredon Bleu and Looks Like Trouble would probably start at a slightly lower price.

The manager jokingly said, 'Well it will certainly look like trouble for one of us; either for me, who will lose over half a million pounds, or you, who will lose your friends' money.'

The Major thanked him and they made their way to the second bookmakers where the negotiations were repeated exactly. Jerry said that it was quite clear that the Major was not only known but respected, and he felt very confident that the exercise would be a big success. Before returning to Hollytree House they called in at their local pub and drank a toast to the success of the Cheltenham Four.

*

Unfortunately, Tricia received some very disturbing news. It seemed that Mr James, one of the residents removed as a group of three, had not liked his new home. He kept walking out saying that he was going back to Hollytree House. The staff at his new home decided that the only way to cope with this was by tying him into the chair in his bedroom. He was usually taken downstairs for his meals but one lunchtime he had been forgotten and nobody went to collect him until the evening meal. When a member of staff went up to his room she found that he was dead. He had apparently tried to wriggle down under the ropes and had in the process strangled himself.

Tricia discussed the tragedy with Paula and Tim and they again decided that there was not much point in informing the residents. 'Poor Mr James would definitely still be enjoying his life here if they had left him alone,' Tricia said angrily.

Chapter Fifty-Nine

Thursday was a bright, clear morning and the Major thought, 'Well by this time next week we should be on the last leg of the accumulator.' In the afternoon he and Jerry went to Tricia's office for their meeting with Mr Khan. The Major had spoken to Tricia during the morning and explained that they would have to be rather vague with Mr Khan about where the money would be coming from. Tricia wasn't entirely happy about this as she didn't want Mr Khan to be misled with any false optimism. The Major assured her that they would simply ask Mr Khan for a short period of time before finalising their offer.

Mr Khan arrived at about three o'clock and Tricia asked the Major if he and Jerry wanted her to sit in on the meeting. He assured her that they did because the future would very much depend on her involvement. Mr Khan looked just as worried as he had on Monday. He and Tricia explained about the meeting with the Social Services and told the Major and Jerry that they saw no point in appealing against the decision. The Major said that he understood this and that was why he and Jerry had asked to meet Mr Khan. He then went on to ask Mr Khan if he would be prepared to consider selling Hollytree House to a committee of the residents.

Mr Khan was somewhat taken aback. 'Oh my goodness,' he said, 'I didn't think for one minute that this was the reason you had asked for a meeting.' He then went on to say that he'd already had an offer for the sale of the house.

Tricia interrupted at this point and said, 'I bet the offer was from Jack Smith.'

'That's right,' said Mr Khan. 'How did you know?'

Tricia said that her husband had been making some very discreet enquiries and it appeared that Jack Smith and others had been negotiating with the development company who were planning to build on the land next door.

'That's it,' said the Major. 'That's what all this trouble has been about. It's obvious that Smith is in league with that swine, James Slighe, and the whole plan to close Hollytree House is because they want to acquire the land for development.'

'In which case,' said Jerry, 'all the residents would be turfed out and God knows where we would all finish up.'

Mr Khan said that such accusations would be very difficult to prove and that they should be careful not to create more trouble and find themselves in court for libel or slander.

'Nevertheless,' said Tricia, 'it does all make sense. We have known all along that the charges against us were false and ridiculous but we have been unable to do anything about it.'

Mr Khan then said, 'Of course I may get an offer from the developers but I promised my mother I would keep the homes open for as long as the elderly residents needed them. If a man cannot keep a promise to his mother then he is not worth much, so if you want to buy Hollytree House, have you got the money and how much are you offering?'

The Major said that obviously they would pay as much as Jack Smith had offered and perhaps a little more for the fixtures and fittings.

Mr Khan explained that he had originally hoped for half a million pounds but that Jack Smith had offered four hundred and fifty thousand.

The Major said, 'Supposing we look for a compromise and offer you four hundred and seventy-five thousand pounds?'

Mr Khan agreed that this would be a satisfactory offer but

then asked when the Major and his committee would be able to complete a contract.

The Major looked at his watch and saw that it was four o'clock. 'In exactly one week's time,' he said, thinking to himself that the Gold Cup race would have just been completed.

'If not,' said Mr Khan, 'then I will probably have no choice but to accept Smith's offer as I have now made plans to return to Pakistan.'

Chapter Sixty

After Mr Khan left, looking considerably more cheerful than when he arrived, the Major asked Tricia if he and Jerry could develop their plans with her. She said that she was only too happy to do this because obviously there were implications for her and other members of staff. Jerry said that he and the other members of the committee had discussed the future of a possible commune and it was quite clear that the residents would not be able to manage on their own.

He went on to say that they had all agreed that they would ask Tricia to stay on as the manager of the commune and if their plans came to fruition they would be able to pay her the same salary as she was receiving at present. Tricia was very pleased to hear this but pointed out that she would of course need other staff to support her. 'Yes indeed,' said Jerry, 'and we have discussed this very carefully and would like your opinion.' He went on to say that if Tricia agreed and the other staff were interested in the arrangement they would like to keep Tim and June, assisted by Andy, on a part time basis, and Lucy the cleaner. 'We think,' he said, 'that with that amount of support we should manage very well.'

Tricia thought about if for a moment and said, 'Well Paula and a couple of the other staff have already handed in their notice so it does seem that you have selected the staff that would be most suitable.'

The Major then said that they also proposed to give five

thousand pounds to Bridie so that she could go back to Ireland with her sons. Tricia thought this was a very kind idea and she was sure that Bridie would be delighted. 'All we need now is the money,' said Jerry, 'and by this time next week we will know whether it is available.'

Tricia laughed and said, 'Well I have never been offered employment which was dependent on the result of a horse race before.'

'Four horse races,' said the Major. 'And for me,' he went on, 'the fulfilment of a lifetime's ambition.'

Jerry then suggested to Tricia that they should have a meeting on the following day with the staff they had mentioned and make sure that they too would be happy about the arrangement. Tricia said that she thought that was a good idea and she was fairly certain that they would be very happy about the suggestion. 'I know that none of them actually want to leave,' she said, 'any more than I do, but it will be such an anti-climax if your plans collapse.'

The Major said that he fervently hoped that the plans would not collapse, he somehow felt sure that this year was to be the year when he would achieve his ambition.

Chapter Sixty-One

The meeting with the staff duly took place on Friday, although there was no point in mentioning their idea to Bridie at this stage in case she had to be disappointed. Tim and Andy were very enthusiastic about the idea and Tim said how much more interesting life could be for the residents without the constraints imposed by Social Services. When Tricia pointed out that there would be no money forthcoming from Social Services the Major told them that they had taken this into account in their budget.

The weekend passed in a flurry of excitement; all the Sunday papers were seized and the information about the Cheltenham Festival was read avidly by everyone, even those residents who knew nothing about horse racing. On Monday morning the doorbell rang and when Tim answered it he was confronted by James Slighe and Miss Burley. Slighe asked to see Tricia and said that he had come to remind her that the home would have to close in just over two weeks' time. He asked if she had started to make plans for moving the remainder of the residents. Tricia told him that she was well aware of the official closing date and that she was holding discussions with the residents.

Slighe then said that he assumed Tricia would not mind if he and Miss Burley had a look round and spoke to the residents. Tricia said that at this stage she obviously could not prevent him from looking round but she would have to ask the residents whether they wished to see him. She went into the sitting room and told the residents of Slighe's request. They were very angry and unanimous in their agreement that they did not wish to see him. Jerry accompanied Tricia into the hall and told Slighe that they had formed a residents' committee and none of them wished to see him or hear him. Obviously he could not force himself upon them so he left with Miss Burley saying to Tricia, 'It will be a good job when this place is closed down.'

Slighe went back to his office where he proceeded to write out his resignation. He took it into the Director and explained that he thought there would be some unpleasant publicity about the closure of Hollytree House and that therefore it was a good time for him to move on. The Director was surprised at the news and for the first time began to wonder if there had been any ulterior motive behind the pressure which Slighe had put on Hollytree House. He asked Slighe what his plans were and Slighe told him that he and his wife were thinking about buying a property in France and opening a small hotel for English tourists. The Director wished him good luck and said he would be glad when he too could retire. Slighe was a bit surprised and disappointed that the Director had accepted his resignation so readily but then he thought about almost a million pounds and smiled happily to himself as he left the Director's office.

*

That night, on the eve of the Cheltenham Festival, the Major could not sleep. He reminisced that the last time he had felt so apprehensive was in 1944. Then he had been a very young subaltern sitting in a landing craft heading for what had been designated as Sword Beach. There were shells bursting all around the craft and the chatter of machine gun and small arms fire was constant and deafening. He had felt both excited and terrified and just hoped that he would survive. Survive he did, not only then, but later in the trenches in Korea and the jungle in Malaysia. The present situation was somehow different but worse, the future happiness and well-being of his fellow residents was dependent on his wild gamble. After a long time he fell asleep and woke in a cold sweat, having dreamt that the first three horses won and then Looks Like Trouble had fallen at the first fence. He was very relieved when it was time for breakfast.

CHAPTER SIXTY-TWO

Tuesday afternoon found all the residents sitting around the television watching in a feverish state of excitement. When Istabraq won the Champion Hurdle like an odds on chance should, there was a great roar and everybody started talking excitedly. The Major pointed out that they shouldn't get too excited yet because that was the easiest leg of the accumulator. For his part he had one of the blinding headaches which he had been getting ever since his mishap, and after dinner he withdrew to his room. Wednesday afternoon was a repeat of the day before. Everyone gathered round the television and at the start of the Queen Mother Champion Chase there were shouts of, 'Come on Blue Bedspread, you can do it.' The residents cheered at every jump and sure enough Edredon Bleu did do it, and the residents were half way there in their attempt to save Hollytree House.

On Wednesday evening the whole house seemed to be tense with excitement. The residents behaved as if they did not know what to do with themselves and could not settle. Neither bridge nor liar dice had any appeal and Tim and Tricia spent all their time trying to keep the residents calm. The only people who were unaffected were Mrs Robertson and Miss Ellis, both of whom were slightly bewildered about the excitement affecting the rest of the residents. Eventually most of the residents retired to their room by eleven-thirty but Tricia saw that many of their lights were still burning long after midnight. She had decided to sleep in due to the excitement, and rang her husband to tell him about the situation. Robbie was as calm as always and told her that he was sure everything would work out for the best. She eventually drifted off to sleep hoping he was right.

On Thursday morning the Major asked Tricia if he could address both residents and staff at coffee time. He said that the first race on the afternoon's programme was the Triumph Hurdle and he fervently hoped that Willy's hunch about Snowdrop would be proved right. The Gold Cup was the third race and he reminded them that Looks Like Trouble was the final leg of their accumulator. He also told them that he had asked both bookmakers to respect their confidentiality. 'There is no need for anyone except us and Mr Khan to know if we are successful,' he said. Jerry said that he was sure it would all leak out eventually but the Major replied that eventually would be alright. 'After we've told Smith and Slighe,' he added with a chuckle.

He then told them about the two hundred pounds which he had kept back for the party. He said that Tim had volunteered to take people into town so that some of the ladies could go to the supermarket for food and the men to the wine merchants for drinks. 'It will either be a glorious celebration or a wake,' he said. The bridge ladies volunteered to get the food and Glyn and Jerry said that they would get the drinks. Vic said that he would do his best to keep the Major calm and everyone laughed because the Major seemed to be the calmest person in the room. In fact he had another of his headaches and some considerable anxiety about their choice in the Triumph.

However, at two o'clock everyone gathered in the sitting room and loudly shouted Snowdrop home in the Triumph Hurdle. There were lots of kisses and congratulations for Willy and the Major and then after numerous visits to the toilet they all settled down to watch the Gold Cup at three-thirty.

The horses were restless at the start and twice the starter

asked them to take a turn and come in again. Eventually they were off and the residents were on the edge of their seats, urging Looks like Trouble and jockey, Richard Johnson, over every fence. As they crossed the fifth fence the horse stumbled slightly. Willy screamed and everyone else in the room held their breath. As the horses thundered up the final hill the excitement was unbearable and the shouts and screams brought a terrible pain to the Major's head. When Looks like Trouble was announced the winner everyone went wild but the Major simply sat quite still, aware only of the thunderous noise in his head. Several of the residents approached him and asked if they had definitely won the money. All the Major could do was to nod and grit his teeth.

Chapter Sixty-Three

Sometime later Jerry reminded the Major that they had to contact Mr Khan. They went into Tricia's office and asked her if she would telephone Mr Khan and confirm that they were in a position to pay the agreed four hundred and seventy-five thousand pounds. Tricia was in a daze and couldn't believe that it was actually going to happen. However, she dialled Mr Khan's number and he must have been waiting by the telephone because he picked it up after the first ring.

When Tricia confirmed the sale he was absolutely delighted. They agreed that as there was going to be no mortgage involved they could complete by the following Friday. The Major then asked Tricia to request Mr Khan to keep the news confidential until the sale was completed. Mr Khan said, 'What, not even Jack Smith?'

'Especially Jack Smith,' Tricia confirmed. 'The residents' committee would like to call a meeting here a week tomorrow and would be glad if you could come, but not a word until then.'

Mr Khan promised his silence apart from getting his solicitors to produce the necessary documents in time for the meeting.

All three of them then went back into the sitting room and over a much-needed cup of tea the Major again stressed the importance for secrecy for the next eight days. Miss Ellis made them all laugh by saying that she would find it very hard to keep a secret if she didn't know what the secret was. Tricia decided to take her and Mrs Robertson to one side and gently explain the situation. Jerry and the Major said that they would go to the bookmakers on the following morning and collect the two cheques for well over a million pounds. It was agreed that they would then deposit them in a bank account for which Jerry and Harriet would be the joint signatories.

*

The party that night was riotous. Most of the residents got quite merry and many of them were still enjoying themselves well past midnight. When Tricia expressed some concern about their well-being, Robbie and Tim said that it was such an amazing and momentous occasion, a little risk was justified. Nevertheless Tricia was relieved when they eventually all went to their beds and the house became silent.

Chapter Sixty-Four

The next few days saw a number of meetings in Hollytree House. The committee asked Harriet if she would contact her retired solicitor friend and get him to draw up a trust deed so that the house would be vested in all their names. They agreed that there was no need to introduce any more residents as fourteen would give them the extra space to provide en-suite facilities for all the bedrooms. Tim and Andy could do much of the work in order to save costs and Tim had agreed to move into the house on a permanent basis. Tricia, June, Andy and Lucy would continue to come in on a rota basis and one of the cooks, Amy Halliday, had indicated that she too would like to stay on.

It was all very exciting and when on the Wednesday, Tricia called Bridie into the office and gave her five thousand pounds she was first of all speechless and then delighted. Tricia explained that the residents had deducted it from their winnings so that Bridie could go back to Ireland if she wanted. 'If I want,' said Bridie. 'Nothing would please me more, and the boys and I will be off as soon as possible. He won't dare to follow me because my father and brothers would give him a real thrashing.'

Thursday was devoted to planning the meeting on the following day. Mr Khan, Jack Smith and James Slighe had been invited and the music room was turned into a formal meeting room. It was agreed that Jerry, Harriet, Willy and the Major would represent the residents and Tim and Tricia would represent the staff. Jerry rubbed his hands with glee and said, 'They won't know what's hit 'em.' Willy added that she couldn't wait to see their faces.

But wait she must, for the meeting was scheduled for three o'clock and then the residents and staff would exact their revenge for the past few months of misery. Tricia asked the Major how he felt about their success. He said that he was pleased and quoted an old Chinese proverb which said that if a man sits by a river long enough, all his enemies will come floating past. Tricia felt a slight chill at the Major's words and suggested it was time for bed.

CHAPTER SIXTY-FIVE

At ten minutes to three on Friday afternoon the doorbell rang and Mr Khan appeared. Tricia showed him into the music room where the four residents were already seated at one end of a long table. It was actually three tables from the dining room, which had been placed together and covered by a white sheet. Tricia sat Mr Khan down in the middle and shortly afterwards Tim showed in Jack Smith and James Slighe, who sat at the opposite end of the table to the residents. Tricia could not help thinking that it was a bit like the meeting to discuss the de-registration. 'This time, though, the boot is on the other foot,' she thought.

They all sat quietly whilst Tricia and Tim passed around cups of coffee and it was almost as if nobody knew how to start. The tension in the room was palpable with both sides anticipating a different outcome. Then Mr Khan said, 'Well perhaps I should open the proceedings as the main purpose of the meeting is the transfer of Hollytree House.'

Jack Smith said that he, too, understood that the purpose of the meeting was the transfer of the house but he could not understand why there were residents and staff present. 'I suppose Tricia should be here,' he said, 'but I can't imagine what the rest of them are doing.'

'Patience, my friend,' said Mr Khan. 'All will be soon revealed.'

James Slighe said that he could not understand why he had

been invited to the meeting because whoever owned the house would almost certainly not get permission to re-register it.

'Bloody rubbish,' said Jerry. 'We all know damn well that there would be no intention of Jack Smith re-opening the home if he bought it. We have been reliably informed that the plan would be to close the home and sell the land for redevelopment.'

'Which is why,' interceded the Major, 'we have made Mr Khan an alternative offer.'

For a moment there was a stunned silence and then Jack Smith banged on the table, his face a shade of puce. 'You can't renege on our deal, Khan. I made you a fair offer.'

'Ah,' said Mr Khan, 'I never confirmed that I would accept your offer and the residents have made me a better one.'

'How much better,' said Smith, and Mr Khan replied that they were going to pay four hundred and seventy-five thousand pounds. 'In that case,' said Smith, 'We will pay you five hundred thousand pounds.'

'I'm sorry,' said Mr Khan, 'but I have given my word to the residents and they are ready to complete today.'

'This is ridiculous,' shouted James Slighe. 'We will never agree to the re-registration.'

The Major smiled and said, 'Now you see, Tricia, just what all the manipulation and unpleasantness has been about. These two crooks were prepared to ruin the lives of the residents and the careers of the staff just to make themselves money. They are despicable.'

Mr Khan took the document out of his briefcase and slid it across to Jerry. 'The official transfer,' he said. 'It just needs your representatives' signatures.'

Jerry took an envelope from his pocket and passed it to Mr Khan. 'Your cheque, sir,' he said, 'and may I say on behalf of the residents how grateful we are that you are a gentleman.'

'Gentleman!' said Jack Smith. 'He's a double-crossing swine!'

James Slighe said, 'I have already told you, you will never get registration.'

Jerry got to his feet and said, 'You can stuff your registration, this is now the Hollytree Commune and you two creeps are trespassing!' He opened the door and called for Andy and said, 'Will you and Tim kindly show these two apologies for human beings off the premises and warn them not to return.'

'You haven't heard the last of this!' shouted Slighe as he and Smith were pushed none too gently out of the front door.

*

A Major Miracle

Author's Notes

It would be nice to think that all stories have happy endings, with the good people triumphant and the villains getting their just deserts. However, this particular story contains elements of both. On the Tuesday after the Friday meeting, the Director of Social Services received a letter informing him that Hollytree House was now a private establishment and all social workers were persona non grata. On the same day Tim telephoned a reporter friend and gave him an interesting story. It was no coincidence that both these events occurred on April 1st. By the time the story appeared in a well-known Sunday newspaper, Mr Khan had returned to Islamabad where he became a very successful property developer.

Jack Smith had counted his chickens a little too early and put down a deposit on a new house costing three quarters of a million pounds. He had to withdraw from the purchase and consequently lost his deposit. Reuben Jones, in common with most solicitors, did not lose any money and although he lost face he managed to brazen it out.

James Slighe tried to withdraw his resignation, blaming his deputy, Heap, for the problems. Unfortunately for him the Chair of Social Services, having seen the newspaper report, refused to agree to his reinstatement and he moved on to pastures new. There he is doubtless behaving in the same unpleasant way and creating problems for somebody else. Ken Pratt, who was an incompetent part time soldier at the best of times, fell off an obstacle while on an assault course exercise. He survived the fall but broke a leg and a collarbone in the process.

The residents and staff soon settled comfortably into their new lifestyle. Their future was even more firmly secured when the developer gave them a million pounds for a third of their land and agreed to build a seven-foot wall between Hollytree House and the housing development. Vic and Poppy planned a June wedding and much to Jerry's disgust, Glyn and Joyce decided to make it a double wedding.

Unfortunately the Major would not be present at the wedding. At the end of April on a beautiful spring morning he did not come down for breakfast. When Tricia went to investigate she found to her horror that he had died in his sleep. A post mortem subsequently revealed that a blood clot he sustained as a result of the woodshed incident had finally killed him. He was cremated on a sunny May morning. His son and daughter-in-law, who had moved to New Zealand, were not present. As the staff and residents gathered together after the funeral their discussion reflected how much they all cared for him. They decided not to replace him with another resident but to turn his room into a library. Poppy said that she thought he was really an angel who came to help in their hour of need and created a miracle. Jerry said angel or not he had certainly come up trumps and would be sorely missed.

A Major Miracle

Tricia proposed a toast to the Major and his miracle and they all sang For He's a Jolly Good Fellow.

*

Although this book is entirely fictional there are undoubtedly some homes where residents are badly treated and moved for financial reasons. There must be some homes which are as caring and stimulating as Hollytree House but there are many homes where the care could be improved and some which merit very close inspection. Every social worker and relative should make the most careful enquiries before placing a vulnerable, elderly person in a residential or nursing home. However, it is extremely unlikely that anything similar to Hollytree House could ever happen. The reason for this is that somebody somewhere introduced legislation which made inspection of residential homes a national responsibility rather than being left to individual local authorities. Nevertheless, it would be nice to think that there are elderly people throughout the country who could display the same enthusiasm and initiative as the residents of Hollytree House.